MW00965367

Lazy Lions Have Full Bellies

2nd Edition

Lazy Lions Have Full Bellies, 2nd Edition

Jesse Sharpe

Sharpe Publications

New Carrollton, Md.

Lazy Lions Have Full Bellies

2nd Edition

© 2011, 2018

Cover and Book Design by Jesse Sharpe
Editing by Lauren Cates Ransome

All rights reserved.

No part of this book may be reproduced in any form or by any electronic or mechanical means including information storage and retrieval systems, without permission in writing from the author. The only exception is by a reviewer, who may quote short excerpts in a review.

Visit my website at www.sharpebooksonline.com
author@sharpebooksonline.com
Printed in the United States of America

ISBN-13: 978-1981967315
ISBN-10:1981967311

Other Works By The Author

Lazy Lions Have Full Bellies Story Book

Gods Speaks in Haiku

Spirit Seeking Haiku

Because of You

Meditations in Haiku

In a Haiku Meantime

The Intimate Haiku

Hurry Home (war chronicles)

My Afri-bets Learning Book

My ABC 123 Coloring Book

Words Flowing Up South

Yes! From Awareness to Love, 13 Affirmations in Haiku

"I AM!" Affirmations in Haiku

The Haiku of War

The Secret of Successful Leadership, Vols. I and II

Transformations: From Males to Men

The Seven Principles of Chapter Success: Tapping the Power Within Your Organization

Dedication

All praises to the Creator, through which all good things are made possible. By shining the light inward, I am able to see the God within me.

This book is dedicated to my elders, whose collected wisdom is one of the treasures from which I draw upon to guide me through life. I am but an ant in this struggle, and the mountain ahead, a mere anthill that my ancestors have both built and traveled before. What appears new is usually some variation of something lost, something forgotten, something old, or something that needs remembered. In honor of those who have transitioned, and when called upon will point to the lost, the forgotten, and the old so that we can remember, I say, *Ase. (pronounced, Ah Shey).*

To my grandparents, William and Alberta Sharpe, *Ase*

To my fathers, Jesse Lee and Garland Preston, *Ase*

To a fellow teacher and friend, Baba Kamau Robinson, *Ase*

To a mentor and friend, Michael Amerson, *Ase*

To my mentor, mother and teacher, Queen Mother Aziza Jones, *Ase*

To all of those whose names are missing from this page, know that you are not forgotten, and that your names resonate in my heart. To you, I say, *Ase*

Contents

Chapter 6 – War and Conflict............................. **77**

Chapter 7 – Wealth, Money, Greed, and Thieves............... **95**

Chapter 8 – Cowards, Pride, and Fools........................... **107**

Chapter 9 – Fear and Faith **117**

Introduction

Lazy Lions Have Full Bellies is a collection of African folktales and proverbs that re-introduces the wisdom of African wisdom to listeners of all ages. I use the word "re-introduce" because in the spirit of Sankofa, which in Twi translates to "go back and get it", the reader is being taken back to reclaim and secure something important that has been left behind. In this case, the objects to be fetched are the priceless pearls of wisdom that are found in African folktales and proverbs. Parents, teachers, and mentors will not have any difficulty in finding the right story or the perfect idiom to spark nurturing and dynamic conversations with their students and mentees. For children in primary school, there is also a *Lazy Lions Have Full Bellies Storybook*.

Inseparable from traditional African culture, African folktales and proverbs tackle a broad range of socio-historical and political issues. The most preferred method of transmitting this knowledge is through word of mouth, or to borrow a more modern term attributed to poetry, the spoken word. Mistaken as humorous nonsense stories for children, folktales and proverbs deliver moral and character instruction to the listener, as well as historical and cultural knowledge that helps to explain the way things came to be. Folktales are short, fictional narratives that attempt to explain some aspect of life and how things come to be in the world. Making great use of allegories and symbolism, African folktales serve to impart wisdom and lessons of survival, and using wit and folly, the call and response of African folktales transmit and reinforce tradition, history, and cultural morays from one generation to the next. Proverbs are similar; what folktales do in story form, proverbs make up with short phrases called idioms, which tend to focus on generational wisdom and character development that, as with African folktales, often leave the listener befuddled.

Crafted to be passed down through generations by word of mouth, unfortunately African folktales and proverbs have become a casualty of society's self-absorbance into the digital age where children, in particular, spend enormous amount of hours glued to electronic devices that dampen their ability to imagine. Lost within this digital vacuum is the importance of the African storyteller. The griots, jeli, guewel, gawlo, igawen, and gnawi, as they are known in other languages, are the dream weavers, poets, teachers, ministers, advisors, and historians.

Introduction

The voice of the African storyteller may be found lifted in spirit by the background beats of African drums. Europeans call this creative force, God, while the Mande of Senegal and Mali refer to it as Nyama. In an interview with CNN, the late, world-renowned African griot, Sotigui Kouyaté stated that, "Rightly or wrongly, they call us masters of the spoken word. Our duty is to encourage the West to appreciate Africa more. It's also true that many Africans don't really know their own continent. And if you forget your culture, you lose sight of yourself." Kouyaté continues to say, "The day you no longer know where you're going, just remember where you came from… Our strength lies in our culture. Everything I do as a storyteller, a griot, stems from this rooting and openness."

Though rooted in openness, African folktales and proverbs deliver coded messages on many levels. The initial meaning is the outer cloaking. Without an understanding of the true purpose of the folktale, the listener (or reader) enjoys the tale at face value while minimizing, if not wholly ignorant to, its socio-political purpose. Thus, the initial message truly does appear hilarious to children who may need to be entertained or put to sleep, as well as foreigners who the message is purposely hidden from.

Jomo Kenyatta's "The Jungle and the Gentleman" provides a

prime example of what appears to be a nonsensical "folktale" about a man who is pushed out of his house by an elephant. According to the story, an elephant asks an African if he could just stick his trunk into the man's house to keep it from getting wet from the rain. Though suspicious, the African reluctant agrees. Soon after, the arrogant elephant's massive body follows and the elephant not only pushes the African out of his house, but summarily claims the house as his. On one level, this story is nonsensical, because everyone knows, animals can't talk. On a social level, the story makes commentary on trust, following one's intuition, and knowing the character of an individual before they are invited into your home. On an historical level, Kenyatta's folktale comments on historical imperialism and modern-day gentrification.

As with African folktales, similar coded and befuddling messages are found in African proverbs. The proverb, "when lions are not hunting, they are not hungry," has very little to do with the eating habits of lions. This particular proverb is the inspiration for the title of this book, *Lazy Lions Have Full Bellies*, as well as the folktale of the same name. On one level, the proverb warns that appearances can be deceiving, on another it teaches that the enemy, even when it appears docile and weak, is always scheming on ways in which to remain in power.

Introduction

It is precisely due to words having power that African folktales and proverbs are important. Nonsense stories are often the clouds of wisdom, and words on wings of birds flying in the wind are the messengers. The message written in (John 1:1, KJV) of the Bible is that in the very beginning was the Word, "and the Word was with God, and the Word was God." However, centuries before, Man, know thyself, and to thyself be true was inscribed upon the stone Temple of Luxor in Kemet, otherwise known as Egypt. Moving from the east coast of Africa to its west, Ghanaians point out that one lie spoils a thousand truths. In Mauritanian a similar proverb advises, a cutting word is worse than a bowstring, a cut may heal, but the cut of the tongue does not. From Senegal, we are reminded that words are like spears, once they leave your lips they can never come back. And from the Yoruba, it is said that you may tell little lies, small as a thorn, but they will grow to the size of a spear and kill you.

As you might imagine, traditional African culture takes exception to the western expression, sticks and stones may break my bones but words will never hurt me. The power and respect of words that come out of a person's mouth are a result of an African tradition that honors the messenger as much as the message. Westerners teach that the two should remain separate and distinct, for what if the messenger is killed? Though true, it misses the point and devalues the messenger who is entrusted with the message. Because so much in traditional Africa was dependent on the oral tradition, the speaker or messenger's honor, integrity was always important. If he or she was not believable, the message had no power of influence. This is why the jeli (African storyteller) whose total presence, dressed in African garb and accompanied sometimes by drum and dancers, cannot be separated from the folktale or proverb. Additionally, the more that the African storyteller "wows" their listeners, the more of the coded message is transmitted and seeps into the attuned ear.

African folktales and proverbs therefore are food for thought. As with the cooking of any good meal, the aroma rising from the pot will have the hungry listener running to the table. However, the hidden meanings should be chewed slowly, or as we say, marinated on a bit. This is because wisdom, like an elephant, is best eaten in small bites, as little by little becomes a lot. According to African tradition, as with food, knowledge and wisdom are meant to be shared with the entire village because wisdom is like a baobab tree; no one individual can embrace it.

Asanta sana

Chapter 1 – Words of Wisdom

The Pot of Wisdom (An Anansi Folktale)

Once upon a time, when the world was young and animals could talk, Kweku Anansi collected all the wisdom in the world in a large pot. To keep the pot post safe, Kweku Anansi hung it around his neck with rope. With so much to say and share, the pot of wisdom jingled nosily and drew so much attention. Mindful of all the jealous stares, Kweku Anansi said to himself one day, "Now, that I have all the wisdom of the world for myself, I am afraid that these jealous animals will steal it from me."

That night, with thoughts of how to keep the pot of wisdom to himself, Kweku Anansi slept and dreamed of climbing a very tall tree. The next morning, the first thing Kweku Anansi did when he woke up was carefully lift the lid of the pot. He was careful to lift it just a little or all the wisdom in the world might spill out. He then dipped his finger. "Ah ha," he said to himself, "this wisdom is as sweet as honey. I shall hide the pot on top of the tallest tree in the forest."

Such goodness and wisdom, Anansi the spider thought to himself, would only be wasted among the other animals. So, as soon as he finished licking his fingers, he called to Ntikuma, his only son. With walking stick and the pot of wisdom hanging around his neck, off the two went deep into the forest into Anansi until Anansi came upon what looked to be the tallest tree in the world. "Here is where I will safely keep my pot of wisdom," Anansi said to Ntikuma. "This will be our secret to what makes me the wisest in all the world."

With that said, and with the pot hanging around his neck, Anansi attempted to climb the tall tree. However, time after time, with the cumbersome pot swinging from his neck, he tumbled back down to earth. After watching his father's frustrated attempts, Ntikuma sat down next to his father and said, "Father, you have taught me well, so may I offer a suggestion." With both his pride and bottom hurt from his many falls, Anansi nodded and waited to hear what his son had to say. Rubbing his chin, Ntikuma smiled, thankful for the opportunity. His suggested to his father that he hang the pot from his back while climbed what had to be the tallest tree in all the world. "That way," Ntikuma, said, "father, you will be able to climb the tree and be the wisest in all the world as well."

Anansi was proud of his son's wisdom, and followed his son's instructions. When he finally reached the top of the tree, he sat on the topmost branch and rested. It was when he spotted his son far below, with no one to share his pot of wisdom, Anansi said to himself, "I thought I had all the wisdom in the world, but what good is it with no one to share it with. "Also," he hummed to himself, "I thought I had it all in my pot, but my own son, little Ntikuma, has wisdom that I don't have in my pot."

Kweku Anansi sat high up in the tree for a long time, reflecting on what he should do next with his pot of wisdom. It was then that Owl flew overhead and shouted down to him, "Anansi, my dear friend, why are you sitting way up in that tree?"

"Sticking my fingers in my clay pot," Anansi shouted back. "You know it contains all the wisdom in the world."

"All the wisdom in the world?" hooted Owl from a great distance. "Does it contain the secret of flying?"

"Hmm," Anansi pondered. "Let us just see." Anansi dipped his finger into the pot, but no matter how much he licked, he was unable to grow wings like his friend, Owl's. "I don't think so," Anansi shouted back to Owl. "I can no more fly today than I could yesterday."

Words of Wisdom

Circling high above Anansi, Owl chuckled. "My dear friend, Kweku Anansi, wisdom is like the tree you are sitting in; no one person can embrace all of it." As Owl flew off, Anansi could hear his friend laughing, "How stupid of you Kweku Anansi, everyone knows that."

Frowning, Anansi indeed felt foolish. "You are right," Anansi agreed, waving goodbye to his friend, Owl, "wisdom is a thing shared, not hoarded."

Declaring never to be so foolish again, Anansi started climbing back down the tree, but halfway down the tree, the pot slipped from around his neck and smashed to a million pieces on the jungle floor. When the pot smashed open, a millions honeybees came buzzing out and chased Anansi all the way back to their village. Afraid of being stun, Anansi and his son ran so fast they left so much wisdom and knowledge behind.

Something to think about!

Words of Wisdom

African Proverbs

1. Wisdom is like a baobab tree; no one individual can embrace it. (*Ghana, Togo*)
2. From the word of an elder is derived a bone. (*Burundi, Rwanda*)
3. Nobody kills an ignorant person who begs for wisdom. (*Cameroon, Nigeria*)
4. Got a stone but didn't get a nut to crack, got a nut but didn't get a stone to crack it with. (*Ghana*)
5. If a blind man says he will throw a stone at you, he probably has his foot on one. (*Ghana*)
6. Only a wise person can solve a difficult problem. (*Ghana*)
7. There is no medicine against old age. (*Ghana*)
8. Tongue and teeth live in the same house, yet they bite each other. (*Ghana*)
9. What you cannot see during the day, you will not see at night. (*Ghana*)
10. When your mouth stumbles, it's worse than feet. (*Ghana*)
11. You cannot shave a man in his absence. (*Igbo*)
12. If you provoke a rattlesnake, you must be prepared to be bitten by it. (*Kenya*)
13. A messenger cannot be beaten. (*Kenya*)
14. We add wisdom to knowledge. (*Kenya*)

15. The one chased away with a club comes back, but the one chased away with kihooto [reason] does not. (*Kenya*)

16. Tongue and teeth fall out sometimes. (*Liberia*)

17. If you have no teeth, do not break the clay cooking pot. (*Malawi, Tanzania, Zimbabwe*)

18. An elder's stone could miss a bird, but his words of wisdom never fall to the ground. (*Mozambique, Zimbabwe, Zambia*)

19. An old lady cooked stones and they produced soup. (*Mozambique, Zimbabwe, Zambia*)

20. If you do not listen to good advice, you will be embarrassed in public. (*Namibia*)

21. A tree that is no taller than an ant cannot shade you. (*Nigeria*)

22. Proverbs are the palm oil with which words are eaten. (*Nigerian*)

23. It is better to walk than curse the road. (*Senegal*)

24. The teeth of a man serve as a fence. (*Senegal*)

25. Words are like bullets; if they escape, you can't catch them again. (*Senegal, Gambia*)

26. An okra tree does not grow taller than its master. (*Sierra Leone*)

27. Flowing water makes stagnant water move. (*Somalia*)

28. God is a great eye. He sees everything in the world. (*Sudan*)

29. God is our neighbor when our brother is absent. (*Swahili*)

30. Do not insult the hunting guide before the sun has set. (*Tanzania, Mozambique*)

31. Walk on a fresh tree, the dry one will break. (*Tanzania, Mozambique*)

32. When a leaf falls to the ground, the tree gets the blame. (*Tanzania, Mozambique*)

33. The eyes of the wise person see through you. (*Tanzania*)

34. An elder's handbag is never completely empty. (*Uganda*)

35. Water that has been begged for does not quench the thirst. (*Uganda*)

36. A big blanket encourages sleeping in the morning. (*unknown*)

37. A fool is thirsty in the midst of water. (Ethiopia)

38. A loose tooth will not rest until it's pulled out. (Ethiopia)

39. A man's grave is by the roadside. (Ethiopia)

40. A proverb is the horse of conversation: when the conversation lags, a proverb revives it. (*unknown*)

41. A wise man who knows proverbs can reconcile difficulties. (*unknown*)

42. Advise and counsel him; if he does not listen, let adversity teach him. (Ethiopia)

43. As the wound inflames the finger, so thought inflames the mind. (Ethiopia)

44. Before eating, open thy mouth. (*unknown*)

45. Before one cooks, one must have the meat. *(unknown)*

46. Cactus is bitter only to him who tastes of it. (Ethiopia)

47. Confiding a secret to an unworthy person is like carrying grain in a bag with a hole. (Ethiopia)

48. Do not dispose of the monkey's tail before he is dead. *(unknown)*

49. The elder is unable to fight, but he/she has a rich experience for struggles. *(Liberia)*

50. When the blind lead the blind, both shall fall into the ditch. *(African)*

Wisdom, Food, and Wealth (A Nigerian Folktale)

One day Wisdom, Food, and Wealth started on a journey. As they went along, they came upon a man sitting under a tree rubbing his belly. When they asked what he was doing, the man answered that other than being hungry, he was looking for a place to live. "We are also looking for a place to live," they said to the man, "so which of us would you like to take along with you?" At the moment, the man's stomach made a sound like a lion. "I want Food to live with me," the man answered with delight. Fretting, Food said to the hungry man sitting under a tree, "You are a dumb man. If you had chosen Wisdom, all three of us could have lived with you. If I lived with you without wisdom, you could not have me long and we would soon be without a home."

With that said, Wisdom, Food, and Wealth continued on their journey. After a little while, they came upon a tattered clothed woman sitting on a rock. "Woman," the three asked, "why are you out here all alone looking so sad?" Similar to the man they had recently left, the woman answered that she was also looking for a home. Saying they too were looking for a home, Wisdom, Food, and Wealth asked the impoverished woman to choose one of them to help build her home. "I believe," the woman happily said, "that I would like to have Wealth live with me." Groaning, Wealth stomped his foot. "Foolish woman, you are not clever at all. If you had chosen Wisdom, all of us would live with you. I know that without Wisdom I would not last a day in your household. No, you cannot keep me," Wealth groaned.

After leaving the woman with a few words of wisdom to help ponder her unwise decision, Wisdom, Food, and Money continued on. After a day's journey, the three came upon a man and a woman building a hut. "What are you doing?" they asked the couple. The man and the woman looked up from their laboring work and wiped their brow. Before answering, they thought enough to offer

Wisdom, Food, and Wealth a drink of water. "Thank you,"
Wisdom, Food, and Wealth said after sipping from the gourd.
"Now, what are you two doing?" they repeated.

"We are building a place to live," the man and woman replied.

"Is that so?" Wisdom, Food, and Wealth responded.

"Yes," the man and woman smiled, enjoying the brief break in
their work. "It is a small hut, but it will be our home."

"Well then," Wisdom, Food, and Wealth answered in unison,
"if given the choice, which one of us would you like to stay and
live with you?"

Before answering, the couple considered many things. Their
hut would indeed be small, and they had little food. Out of
kindness, however, they answered, "We would like for all three of
you to stay with us. However, since we can only choose one," they
sadly said looking at the other two, "we would like for Wisdom to
live with us."

The couple's answer caused Food to smile happily. "Since you
have chosen Wisdom, then I will also live with you, too. I know
that you will be able to take good care of me." In agreement,
Wealth cheerfully echoed. "And since you have chosen Wisdom, I

too, shall live with you. With Wisdom, we know that you will be able to take good care all of us."

Though the man and woman knew it would be crowded in their little hut, they happily agreed to have Wisdom, Food, and Wealth come live with them as soon as they completed building their house. To the couple's surprise, in a blink of an eye, the hut they had been working on all morning suddenly appeared. In addition, other huts soon sprang up around them, and the couple was much admired and loved for their wisdom, generosity, and faithfulness to each other.

Something to think about!

Chapter 2 – Character and Responsibility

The Cow Tail Switch (A West African Folktale)

One day, after many days of being gone, a great warrior, also a husband and father, did not return from a hunt. Knowing the dangers of the wilderness, with equally great sadness the man's family gave him up for dead. The man's wife cried all night and day at the loss of her husband, fearing for sure that some lion had devoured him. The hunter's three sons felt the same and comforted their mother, but it was the youngest son who continuously cried out, "Where is my father? Where is my father?"

After three days of their mother's wailing, and the youngest son continuously asking, "Where is my father? Where is my father?" the three sons left their mother and went in search for him. They had been gone but one day when they found their father's broken spear and his pile of bones. Though they were glad they had found the remains of their father, they were also sad that his life had come to an end.

Character and Responsibility

Looking down upon the pile of brittle bones, the youngest son cried, "Where is my father? Where is my father?" Remembering what his father had taught him back in the village, the oldest son spoke, "Even though he is dead, I know how to put his bones back together." After the eldest son collected and correctly put them back together in the correct order. The three sons stood vigil around their father's bones, but when the magic did not seem to work, they all fell fast asleep.

In the morning, seeing their father's bones had taken their correct form, the second oldest son said, "Now, with my magic I can put flesh on our father's bones." After the second son used his magic to form flesh on their father's skeleton, again they stood vigil around their father's bones. As happened before, the magic did not work until all three were fast asleep.

On the third day, when the three sons woke up, they all saw there was flesh upon their dead father's lifeless pile of bones. The three sons waited a whole day for their father to rise and walk back to the village with them. Eventually, believing that no amount of magic could bring their father back to life, the two older boys gave up hope, picked up their spears and shields, and said to the youngest son, "Let's take our father's dead body back to our mother so she can see for herself that he is dead."

The youngest son picked up his small spear and shield as well, but then fell upon his father's lifeless body and cried, "We have found our father, we have found our father." At that very instant their father opened his eyes and slowly stood up to his full, regal height. One by one, he hugged all three of his sons and thanked them for using their wonderful magic. "Let's return to the village," he then pronounced, "so that your mother can be happy and sing again."

Upon seeing her husband and three sons enter the village, "There you are my husband," she cried with joy. "Your sons have found you." After much kissing, hugging, and declarations of love, the wife then cooked a hearty meal to put some more meat on her husband's skin and bones. When the boy's father sat down with his family, they could tell that he was truly famished. While he ate, and throughout the night, he retold to his wife, three sons, and whoever came to visit, the story about how Simba, the great lion, had bested him and how his three sons had used their magic to gather up his bones, put skin on them, and bring him back to life. Of course, his three sons had wanted to go right out and kill Simba, but to them their father said, "This day, the lion must have the best part of the story. Let it be so."

Character and Responsibility

According to the custom, the husband and father remained inside his house for four days. On the fifth day, his head was shaven. On the sixth day, he killed a cow and decorated the cow's tail. When the people of the village saw the cow tail switch, all agreed it was very beautiful. On the seventh day, the village held a ceremony to officially welcome the warrior, husband, and father back to the village. There was plenty of food, dancing, and singing during the ceremony, and as there always is when warriors gather around, there was much boasting and retelling of old stories.

After all of the other men had become exhausted with their unbelievable stories, it was time for the boys' father to give an account of his battle with Simba, the great lion.

"Harsh world, this world," the boy's father said to those gathered around to hear how the lion had bested him. "If I had not stepped on old Simba's tail," he laughed ending his story, "I am sure he would not have been so mean to me." The village laughed along with the father for they all knew that *even a mouse will bite if you step on his tail.*

Soon it was time for the father to give the beautiful cow tail switch to one of his sons. Wanting it to enhance their own magic, the two eldest sons argued who's magic had been the most powerful. Each, felt what he had done to bring their father back to life was most important. Though it was clear to everyone that the man's two son's had done a great, magical deed, many were surprised when the father handed the cow tail switch to the youngest son. The father praised both his sons, for truly without their magic he would still be a pile of bones. "However," he declared, "I will give my cow tail switch to my youngest son, for it was his powerful words, 'Where is my father? Where is my father?' that led you all to me. You see," the grateful father, husband, and warrior reminded everyone who had gathered in the circle, "a man is never truly dead, until he is forgotten!"

Something to think about!

African Proverbs

1. The beer is difficult to strain. (*Benin, Ghana, and Togo*)
2. Do not vacillate or you will be left in between doing something, having something, and being nothing. (Ethiopia)
3. One who sees something good must narrate it. (*Uganda*)
4. A stranger does not skin a sheep that is paid as a fine at a chief's court. (*Ghana*)
5. As you worship plantain, remember to worship banana as well. (*Ghana*)
6. No one can corrupt you unless you are corrupt. (*Ghana*)

7. When the bag tears, the shoulders get a rest. (*Ghana*)

8. Where the leopard is made judge the goat will never get a fair judgment. (*Gikuyu*)

9. He who fights a mad man, himself is mad. (*Igbo*)

10. The bush in which you hide, rustles. (*Kenya*)

11. Those who procrastinate never do what they say they will do. (*Kenya*)

12. You cannot use a wild banana leaf to shield yourself from the rains and then tear it to pieces later when the rains come to an end. (*Kenya*)

13. The elephant never gets tired of carrying its tusks. (*Liberia*)

14. No matter how long a log stays in the water, it doesn't become a crocodile. (*Mali*)

15. That which has horns cannot be wrapped. (*Mozambique, Zimbabwe, Zambia*)

16. A boisterous horse needs a boisterous bridle. (*Nigeria*)

17. Goodness gets a seat. (*Nigeria*)

18. He who dines with the dogs will eat feces. (*Nigerian*)

19. People know each other better on a journey. (*Plaatje*)

20. A man who dictates, separates himself from others. (*Somalia*)

21. You can help a stranger but never forget your relative. (*Sudan*)

22. A person who is not disciplined cannot be cautioned. (*Tanzania*)

23. One who bathes willingly with cold water does not feel the cold. (*Tanzania*)

24. If you refuse the advice of an elder, you will walk until sunset. (*Tanzania, Mozambique*)

25. The thing that will hurt you will always keep on coming back even if you try to avoid it. (*Tanzania, Mozambique*)

26. Be on the alert, like the red ant that moves with its claws wide open. (*Uganda*)

27. You would not entrust an old cooking pot to the care of a friend or associate. (*Uganda*)

28. A lie runs so quick; it will always pass the truth, then gets tired shortly and the truth always wins at the end of the race. (*Uganda.*)

29. If you do not step on the dog's tail, he will not bite you. (*unknown*)

30. A chick that will grow into a cock can be spotted the very day it hatches. (*unknown*)

31. A good deed is something one returns. (*unknown*)

32. A man who pays respect to the great, paves the way for his own greatness. (*unknown*)

33. A partner in the business will not put an obstacle to it. (Ethiopia)

34. Clothes put on while running, come off while running. (Ethiopia)

35. Don't insult the crocodile until you cross the water. *(unknown)*

36. Even though the old man is strong and hearty, he will not live forever. *(unknown)*

37. Familiarity breeds contempt; distance breeds respect. *(unknown)*

38. He who receives a gift does not measure. *(unknown)*

39. He who wants to barter, usually knows what is best for him. (Ethiopia)

40. Home affairs are not talked about on the public square. *(unknown)*

41. If you don't stand for something, you will fall for anything. *(unknown)*

42. If your house is burning, there is not time to go hunting. *(unknown)*

43. The path is made by walking. *(unknown)*

44. A bad name is like a stigma. *(unknown)*

45. A man should not swallow poison because he is afraid to spit and offend others. *(unknown)*

46. A man that lives near the river will not use spit to wash his hands. *(unknown)*

47. A river not controllable is bound to burst its banks. *(unknown)*

48. A stranger passing by a home, which death has visited, may yet shed a tear! *(unknown)*

49. Being taller than your father does not mean you are older than him. *(unknown)*

50. Character is like smoke, it cannot be hidden. *(unknown)*

The Eagle and the Chicken (An African American Folktale)

One day a young eagle fell from his nest in a tree and was adopted by a motherly hen. The young eagle found a good home with the hen's chicks. In fact, the baby eagle soon believed he was a chick, too, and that all of the other chicks were his brothers and sisters. As with his adopted brothers and sisters, the baby eagle was taught to wait for the farmer to bring out corn for him to peck, and he truly enjoyed running around and sitting in a hole in the ground on sunny days. Life was good for the baby eagle. Even though the baby eagle was clearly much bigger and stronger than his smaller adopted brothers and sisters, who often made fun of his ugly black feathers, the baby eagle was accepted into the chicken family.

Character and Responsibility

Often the little eagle and his adopted brothers and sisters went running under the fence to the grassy cliff, where they would look out to the distant mountains and wonder what might lie on the other side. The baby eagle would dream as well. "One day," he said to his chicken adopted brothers and sisters, "we should go and find out." The chickens laughed at their ugly brother. "We are but chickens," they declared, "not fools. We dare not leave the safety of our barn." With that, they hopped back to the barn and started playing hide and go seek.

Well, one day when the baby eagle was playing in the yard with his adopted brothers and sisters, a huge shadow flew over him. Instinctively, without even looking up, all the small animals, ducks, rabbits, squirrels, and chickens ran into the barn for safety. Having no such instinct, the baby eagle thought it was a game of hide-n-seek. The little chickens cowered in fear and shouted, "Run brother, run!" But it was too late. In a blink of an eye, a large eagle swooped down from the sky, snatched the baby eagle with his talons, and flew away with him.

"What are you doing playing with those chickens?" the large eagle inquired.

"Please don't eat me!" the baby eagle answered, having heard stories of farm animals being taken away and eaten by such big birds. "I am a chicken. Those are my brothers and sisters."

"No, you are not," screeched the elder eagle as he flew higher into the sky. "You are an eagle. You belong in the sky, not on the ground."

"No, I am not," cried the baby eagle, fearing for his life. "I am a chicken. I cluck, I eat corn, and I sit on holes in the ground. I can't even fly."

"Yes, you can little one," the elder eagle told the baby eagle. "You simply were never taught to fly, AND you never tried. My son, you are an eagle, just like me."

Frightened, because the baby eagle had been taught all his life to fear his own kind, he pleaded for his life. "Please let me go back to my brothers and sisters. I am so small and will not be a good meal for you."

The elder eagle shook his head with regret, knowing exactly what to do. "Again, my son," he spoke to the baby eagle, flying now even higher into the sky, "you are not a chicken, to live in a chicken coup, to peck corn, to hop up and down from fences. That is not the life of an eagle."

Still afraid of being eaten, the baby eagle asked the larger eagle to spare him. "Please put me down safely," he asked, "and I will be forever grateful."

The elder eagle laughed and continued to fly toward the very clouds themselves. To the young eagle's amazement, he could still see his adopted family cowering inside the barn. It had never occurred to the little eagle that he saw life through eagle eyes and not chicken eyes. That is why no matter where his adopted brothers and sisters would hide during hide-n-seek, he would always find them.

"It's the heart of an eagle that matters," the elder eagle said to the baby eagle as they circled the mountain that the baby eagle and his chicken brothers admired from the grassy cliff just outside the barnyard. Then, the elder eagle released the baby eagle from his talons. "Spread your wings," he called to the frightened baby eagle, "and fly."

"I can't," the baby eagle cried, tumbling back down to the barnyard. "I am a chicken, and chickens can't fly."

Swooping down alongside the baby eagle, the elder eagle whispered into his ears, "Listen to your heart, son. Spread your wings and fly."

As the little bird continued to fall, the larger eagle flew alongside and whispered into his ear. "Spread your wings and fly." No matter how much the smaller bird cried, the elder eagle kept telling him the truth about himself. Then, just as the baby eagle tumbled past the top of the tree in the yard, instincts took over. The words from the elder bird touched his heart and the younger bird's wings began to unfurl. As his large shadow swooped over the barnyard and flew back into the air, he called to his adopted family. "Hey y'all, look at me. I can fly! I can fly!"

More afraid than ever, the eagle's adopted chicken brothers and sisters ran even deeper into the barn. Catching the breeze under his wings, the baby eagle lifted himself across the rooftops of the barn. "Yes," he shouted aloud, "I can fly!"

"Yes, you can," the elder eagle proudly encouraged. "You were born to fly and to be free. It is an eagle's destiny."

The truth of it all was that the baby eagle's chicken family had always known he was an eagle. Some even dreamed of flying themselves, but most went on about their little chicken lives plucking at corn and breadcrumbs, sitting in holes in the ground, and hoping that the baby eagle would never realize who he was and make them his next meal.

Something to think about!

Chapter 3 – It Takes a Village

Kiigbo Kiigba and the Helpful Spirits (West Africa)

There was a man named Kiigbo Kiigba who lived a very long time ago in a small Yoruba village. Like many of the villagers, he was a hardworking farmer. However, Kiigbo Kiigba was a stubborn man. In fact, Kiigbo Kiigba in Yoruba means "one who does not hear nor accept suggestions".

Like many villages in the ancient Yoruba world, Kiigbo Kiigba's village was inhabited by both people and spirits. To avoid disputes amongst the two groups, a law was passed that enabled spirits to roam the land on certain days. During those days, all villagers were to stay home. Contrary to custom, on the first day that people were supposed to stay in their homes while the spirits roamed, Kiigbo Kiigba went about tilling the land with his hoe and cutlass in preparation for planting his yams. He had been working for a while when he heard spirit voices all around him. "Who are you and what are you doing?" they asked Kiigbo Kiigba.

"I am Kiigbo Kiigba," he answered. "I am tilling my land."

"Alright, we will help you," the voices replied. Suddenly, hundreds of hoes appeared and started to till the land. In a jiffy, the entire farm was tilled and Kiigbo Kiigba returned home satisfied.

On the second day that people were asked to stay home while the spirits were out, Kiigbo Kiigba chose to go to his farm to plant his yams. He had barely started when the voices he heard the day before came around asking, "Who are you and what are you doing?"

"I am Kiigbo Kiigba," he answered, "and I am planting my yams."

"Alright, we will help you", all the voices said, and in a jiffy all the yam seedlings had been planted in neat heaps. Again, Kiigbo Kiigba returned home, satisfied.

On the third day when people were asked to stay home, Kiigbo Kiigba headed to his farm to harvest his yams. As he started to dig up the first yam, the now familiar voices asked, "Who are you and what are you doing?" As had Kiigbo Kiigba answered the previous days, "I am Kiigbo Kiigba, and I am harvesting my yams."

"Alright, we will help you," the voices said, and in a jiffy all of the yams in the farm had been dug up and placed in a big heap.

"Oh, woe is me," Kiigbo Kiigba lamented, suddenly realizing there was not one ripe yam to harvest. "I did not give my yams time to mature and I cannot take them to the market. My entire crop of yams has been ruined by these helpful spirits. Woe is me," Kiigbo Kiigba continued to cry, hitting his head in sorrow. with both hands

As had happened for the last three days, the spirit voice Kiigbo Kiigba inquired, "Who are you and what are you doing?"

"I am Kiigbo Kiigba," Kiigbo Kiigba cried, "can't you see that I am hitting my head in sorrow."

"Alrighty then," the spirit voices announced in unison, "we will help you." Immediately, upon hearing the voices, Kiigbo Kiigba regretted what he had said. Seconds later, a hundred hands appeared out of nowhere and started beating Kiigbo Kiigba on his head. This time when Kiigbo Kiigba returned home, he was being chased by the spirits who took delight in helping him with his sorrow by hitting him on his head.

Something to think about!

It Takes a Village

African Proverbs

1. When mother cow is cropping grass, her young one watches her mouth. (*Nigeria*)
2. The old woman looks after the child to grow its teeth and the young one in turn looks after the old woman when she loses her teeth. (*Benin, Ghana and Togo*)
3. A chicken that keeps scratching the dung hill will soon find the mother's thigh bones. (*Benin, Ghana, and Togo*)
4. If your cornfield is far from your house, the birds will eat your corn. (*Cameroon, Nigeria*)
5. Patience can cook a stone. (*Cameroon, Nigeria*)
6. The tears of the orphan run inside. (*Cameroon, Nigeria*)
7. It is only a male elephant that can save another one from a pit. (*Democratic Republic of Congo*)
8. A fine harvest is not claimed from one's neighbor's field. (*Democratic Republic of the Congo*)
9. Evil enters like a splinter and spreads like an oak tree. (Ethiopia)
10. When you sort out the grains, it becomes pure. (Ethiopia)
11. The child is capable of splitting open the snail, not the tortoise. (*Ghana*)
12. When you are at home, your troubles can never defeat you. (*Ghana*)

13. If you educate a man you educate an individual, but if you educate a woman you educate a family (nation). (*Ghana*)

14. Do good because of tomorrow. (*Ghana*)

15. Dogs do not actually prefer bones to meat, it is just that no one ever gives them meat. (*Ghana*)

16. If nothing touches the palm-leaves they do not rustle. (*Ghana*)

17. The baby who will not let its mother sleep, will itself not sleep either." (*Ghana*)

18. The orphan does not rejoice after a heavy breakfast. (*Ghana*)

19. You don't need a light to see someone you know intimately at night. (*Ghana*)

20. A fly without an adviser, usually follow the corpse to the grave. (*Igbo*)

21. An owl farted and demanded to be praised by his kinsmen, they mocked him that it is not right to dance to an abomination. (*Igbo*)

22. Be ready, for he who lifts up a finger at others, with contempt will surely do same to you. (*Igbo*)

23. A child (young person) does not fear treading on dangerous ground until he or she gets hurt (stumbles). (*Kenya*)

24. What is in the stomach carries what is in the head. (*Kenya*)

25. One who relates with a corrupt person likewise gets corrupted. *(Kenya)*

26. The mother hyena does not eat up all the food. *(Kenya)*

27. A champion bull starts from birth. *(Kenya)*

28. A marriage which has children never ends. *(Kenya)*

29. How easy it is to defeat people who do not kindle fire for themselves. *(Kenya)*

30. One person is thin porridge or gruel; two or three people are a handful of stiff cooked corn meal. *(Kenya)*

31. Slowly, slowly, porridge goes into the gourd. *(Kenya, Tanzania)*

32. The one who milks the cow is not the same person as the one who removes (plucks out) ticks from a cow. *(Kenya)*

33. You cannot take away someone's luck. *(Kenya)*

34. You suffer from smoke produced by the firewood you fetched yourself. *(Kenya)*

35. The small fish employs the name of a large fish when in trouble. *(Kenya, Tanzania)*

36. Smoke does not affect honeybees alone; honey gatherers are also affected. *(Liberia)*

37. Alive, we live in the same house or under the same roof. Dead, we rest in the same tomb. *(Madagascar)*

38. If you sell a drum in your own village, you get the money and keep the sound. *(Madagascar)*

39. A child of the kwale bird learns how to fly. (*Malawi, Tanzania, Zimbabwe*)

40. Before eating the chicken carefully observe the character of your guest. (*Mali*)

41. Although the branch is broken off, the trunk remains. (*Maori*)

42. A child, like the tender bamboo, cannot be used to build a house. (*Mozambique, Zimbabwe, Zambia*)

43. One man cannot surround an anthill. (*Mozambique, Zimbabwe, Zambia*)

44. A weaning baby that does not cry aloud will die on its mothers back. (*Mozambique, Zimbabwe, Zambia*)

45. Eat what you have found with your relatives, non-relatives are forgetful. (*Mozambique, Zimbabwe, Zambia*)

46. If you are ugly you must either learn to dance or make love. (*Mozambique, Zimbabwe, Zambia*)

47. One's neighbors' problems do not induce one to lose one's appetite. (*Mozambique, Zimbabwe, Zambia*)

48. The forest provides food to the hunter after he is utterly exhausted. (*Mozambique, Zimbabwe, Zambia*)

49. When a tree falls on a yam farm and kills the farm's owner, you don't waste time counting the numbers of yam hips ruined. (*Nigeria*)

50. The shield must be prepared long before the fight. (*Nigeria*)

Lion Who Thought He Was Wiser Than His Mother

(South Africa)

Once upon a time when Lion, Man, Baboon, Buffalo and other friends were playing at a certain game, there was a great thunderstorm. Lion and Man began to quarrel. "I shall run to the rain-field," said Lion. "I shall run to the rain-field," countered Man.

As neither would concede this to the other, they separated with much anger. Later that evening, Lion sat around the fire and told his mother what had happened between him and Man. "My son," his mother warned, "beware of Man whose head is in a line with his shoulders and breast, who has stabbing weapons, who keeps white dogs, and who goes about wearing the tuft of a tiger tail. Beware of him!"

Defiant, the brave young lion asked his mother, "Why do I need to be watchful against someone I know? Not only that mother, I am much bigger than Man. And," he added looking down ta her, "I have even grown a bit larger than you."

"Oh, my Son," his mother warned, "take care of him who has stabbing weapons!"

The next morning Lion did not follow his mother's advice. When it was still pitch dark, he went out looking for Man. Just so happens, Man was also out and about. When he spotted Lion, as Lion's mother had foretold, Man let his dogs loose on Lion. It was not until Lion was at the point of death did Man call off his dogs. "Let him alone now," Man ordered, "that he may go and be taught by his Mother."

After being let go, Lion dragged himself home. "Oh mother, take care of me!" he cried out. "I fear I have been gravely wounded."

At dawn, Lion's mother heard his wailing. "My son, she called out to him, "this is the thing which I have told you. Beware of the one who has stabbing weapons and who wears a tuft of tiger's tail. Beware of him who has white dogs, who eats raw flesh, even though you are a flesh-devourer. Son," Lion's mother wept, "did I not tell you beware of the one whose nostrils are red from the prey, even though yours also are blood-stained? Ay, but you did not listen. You thought because you had grown strong and could look down on me that you were wiser than your mother. Oh, my son, now it is I who am looking down on you."

omething to think about!

Chapter 4 – Ambition and Achievement

The Horse and the Ass (An Aesop's Fable)

A Horse and an Ass were travelling together, the Horse prancing along in its fine trappings, the ass carrying with difficulty the heavy weight of its panniers (baskets).

"I wish I were you," sighed the Ass, "having nothing to do and well fed. Look at you with that fine harness. Ahhh, what a life."

The next day there was a great battle and the Horse, not the Ass, led the charge. Well, in the final charge of the day, in its entire splendor, the Horse was mortally wounded. Well, as he lay on the side of the road stripped of his splendor and taking his last breath, his old friend the Ass, happened to pass by pulling an old raggedy cart. Finding his friend the Horse at the point of death, "I was wrong," said the Ass, "better humble security than gilded danger."

Something to think about!

Ambition and Achievement

African Proverbs

1. During the storm, the bird that flies highest sees the dry land. *(unknown)*

2. By trying often, the monkey learns to jump from the tree. *(Cameroon)*

3. A man's wealth may be superior to him. *(Cameroon, Nigeria)*

4. If the wind does not blow, you will not see the chicken's behind. *(Cameroon, Nigeria)*

5. By coming and going, a bird weaves its nest. *(Ghana)*

6. He who pursues a chicken often falls while the chicken continues to run. *(Igbo)*

7. He who refuses to obey cannot command. *(Kenya)*

8. If one is roasting two potatoes, one of them is bound to get charred. *(Kenya)*

9. Beer that will spoil ferments unequally. *(Kenya, Tanzania)*

10. While the sun is shining, bask in it. *(Malawi, Tanzania, Zimbabwe)*

11. One who enters the forest does not listen to the breaking of the twigs in the brush. *(Mozambique, Zimbabwe, Zambia)*

12. Take your chance while opportunity presents itself. (*Mozambique, Zimbabwe, Zambia*)

13. A bird that flies from the ground onto an anthill does not know that it is still on the ground. (*Nigeria*)

14. The earth moves at different speeds depending on who you are. (*Nigeria*)

15. Rising early makes the road short. (*Senegal*)

16. Luck is not a race. (*South Africa*)

17. Not everyone who chased the zebra caught it, but he who caught it chased it. (*South Africa*)

18. The foot has no nose. (*South Africa*)

19. Cows are born with ears; later they grow horns. (*Sudan*)

20. The chief's son has to collect firewood when destiny destroys him. (*Sudan*)

21. A person who does not cultivate well his or her farm always says that it has been bewitched. (*Tanzania*)

22. Suffering is prior to attaining success or perfection. (*Tanzania*)

23. A tutsi liked to warm himself by the fire; someone else took the bull. (*Tanzania, Mozambique*)

24. One who is crazy for meat hunts buffalo. (*Uganda*)

25. The rainmaker who doesn't know what he's doing will be found out by the lack of clouds. (*Uganda*)

26. He who wears too fine clothes, shall go about in rags. *(unknown)*

27. If you do not go out to fish, you have to eat bread. *(unknown)*

28. A bird that is eating guinea-corn keeps quiet. *(unknown)*

29. A bird will always use other birds' feathers to feather its own. *(unknown)*

30. A man with too much ambition cannot sleep in peace. *(unknown)*

31. Around a flowering tree, one finds many insects. *(unknown)*

32. Don't set sail on someone else's star. *(unknown)*

33. He who cannot dance will say: the drum is bad. *(unknown)*

34. He who digs too deep for a fish, may come out with a snake. *(unknown)*

35. He who is unable to dance says that the yard is stony. *(unknown)*

36. Hurry, hurry has no blessing. *(unknown)*

37. Smooth seas do not make skillful sailors. *(Ethiopia)*

38. No one can take another person's mushroom. *(unknown)*

39. No matter how long and staunch a person's neck, on top of it must always sit the head. *(unknown)*

40. Bad dancers blame the dance floor. *(unknown)*

41. A sinking vessel needs no navigation. *(unknown)*

42. Constant thumping softens the hill. *(unknown)*

43. Don't make excuses, make it right! *(unknown)*

44. Doors that open easy, close even easier. *(unknown)*

45. Every door that has a lock always has a key. *(unknown)*

46. A coward has no scar. *(unknown)*

47. A stumble is not a fall. *(Haiti)*

48. The man who builds his own throne rules over a desert. *(Guinean)*

49. To try and to fail is not laziness. *(African)*

50. Little by little an egg will walk. *(Ethiopia)*

The Tortoise Captures the Elephant (West Africa)

Once there was a king who had been trying very hard to capture the elephant for his personal collection, but the elephant had proved elusive. After all the hunters in the kingdom had tried but failed to capture the elephant, the king promised anyone who could capture the elephant half of his kingdom. Well, when the tortoise heard about the reward, he went to the king to accept the challenge. The king was very amused. "All my hunters have failed to capture the elephant and you think you can succeed where they failed?" the king asked. Nodding, with his arms crossed with confidence, the tortoise insisted that he was up to the task and promised to deliver the elephant to the king in two days.

Days later, with a plan in mind, in a path leading into the village, the tortoise dug a hole big enough to hold the elephant captive. After covering the hole with sticks and leaves, he then went to seek out the elephant. Upon finding the elephant in a clearing, he told the elephant, "You know you are the largest animal in the forest and you should be king." The elephant had never considered this before but he thought it was not a bad idea. The tortoise then told the elephant that the villagers had decided to make the largest animal their king and were all expecting the elephant to come to the village and be crowned.

The more the elephant considered being a king, the more excited he became. Then, deciding that being a king was a good thing, he told the tortoise to lead the way. "Great!" the tortoise exclaimed, and then he adorned the elephant with colorful beads. Beating a gong, the tortoise then sang songs praising the elephant as they followed the path into the village. Upon nearing the trap, the tortoise being a much smaller animal, walked lightly over the trap without falling in. The elephant however, who had followed the advice of the tortoise who was singing his praises, fell through the sticks and leaves into the deep hole that had been dug. That was how the tiny tortoise captured the huge elephant and earned one-half of the king's kingdom.

Something to think about!

Chapter 5 – Relationships

Why the Sun and the Moon Live in the Sky

(Nigerian Folktale)

Many years ago, the sun and the water were great friends who lived on the earth together. Very often, the sun would visit the water, but for some reason, the water never returned the sun's visits. Finally, the sun asked the water why he never visited. The water replied that the sun's house was not big enough and that if he came with all his people, he would drive the sun out of his home. Water then said, "If you want me to visit you, you will have to build a very large house. But I warn you that it will have to be very large, as my people are numerous and take up a lot of room."

After a little thought, the sun promised to build a very large house. When he returned home to his wife, the moon, she greeted her husband with a broad smile. The sun told the moon what he had promised the water, and the next day they began building a large house to entertain the water and all his people. When it was completed, the sun asked the water to come and visit him.

Ambition and Achievement

The next day when the water arrived, one of the water's messengers was sent ahead to ask whether it would be safe for the water to enter. Happy that the water came to visit, and sure that there was enough room for all the water, the sun answered, "Yes, tell my friend to come on in." Soon after, the water began to flow in, followed by the fish and all the other water animals. In no time at all the water was knee-deep in the sun's house. Concerned, water asked the sun if it was still safe. Again, the sun said, "Yes," and so more of the water came pouring in.

When the water was at the level of a man's head, the water said to the sun, "Do you still want more of my people to come?" Not knowing any better, the sun and the moon both said, "Yes." So more of the water's people came in. In fact, so many came that the sun and moon had to climb on top of their own roof. Once again the water asked the sun if it was still okay to keep coming in. As they had before, both the sun and moon answered yes. As water rose, soon it overflowed the top of the roof as well and both the sun moon were forced up into the sky. To this very day, both the son and his wife, the moon, sit in the sky to greet water, and they have been there ever since that first meeting.

Something to think about!

Ambition and Achievement

African Proverbs

1. Even though the baby monkey appears so ugly, it's mother loves it anyway. *(unknown)*
2. He who marries a real beauty is seeking trouble. *(Ghana)*
3. If an arrow has not entered deeply, then its removal is not hard. *(Ghana)*
4. So many *little* things makes a man love a woman in a *big* way. *(Ghana)*
5. Bad dancing does not break an engagement. *(Kenya)*
6. Even a friend cannot rescue one from old age. *(Kenya)*
7. Leave bad things, talk peace. *(Kenya)*
8. We should talk while we are still alive. *(Kenya)*
9. A man that does not lie shall never marry. *(Mozambique, Zimbabwe, Zambia)*
10. The word of a friend makes you cry; the word of an enemy makes you laugh. *(Niger)*
11. Hold a true friend with both hands. *(Nigeria)*
12. One does not love if one does not accept from others. *(Nigeria)*
13. If there is cause to love someone, the cause to love has just begun. *(Senegal)*
14. To love the king is not bad, but a king who loves you is better. *(Senegal)*

15. Love is blind. *(Sierra Leone)*

16. One who loves you, warns you. *(Uganda)*

17. A home without a woman is like a barn without cattle. (Ethiopia)

18. A little rain each day will fill the rivers to overflowing. *(unknown)*

19. Absence makes the heart forget. *(unknown)*

20. Dine with a stranger but save your love for your family. (Ethiopia)

21. Hearts do not meet one another like roads. *(unknown)*

22. If the heart is sad, tears will flow. (Ethiopia)

23. If you burn a house, you can't conceal the smoke. *(unknown)*

24. If you tell people to live together, you tell them to quarrel. *(unknown)*

25. It takes two to make a quarrel. *(unknown)*

26. There's no virgin in a maternity ward. *(unknown)*

27. A comb becomes bad when it hurts you. *(unknown)*

28. A good turn deserves another. *(unknown)*

29. A man without a good wife is like a kitchen without a knife. *(unknown)*

30. Feed your deceitful friends with a short spoon and they will bite your fingers. Feed them with a long spoon and they can't bite your fingers. *(unknown)*

31. Good cooking is a woman's surest path to a man's heart. *(unknown)*

32. He, who marries a beauty, marries trouble. *(unknown)*

33. He, who marries a woman only for her beauty, has ignored a major part of what makes a woman. *(unknown)*

34. If a bachelor decides to cook and at the same time goes to climb the palm tree, if he does not fall from the palm tree, his food on the fire (stove) will get burnt. *(unknown)*

35. If the chicken attacks you in the morning, run, because it may have grown teeth overnight. *(unknown)*

36. If your mouth turns into a knife, it will cut off your lips. *(unknown)*

37. It is an act of cowardice for a husband to ask his wife to go and fetch water while he buys akara balls. *(unknown)*

38. It is better to travel alone than with a bad companion. *(unknown)*

39. It is not with saying, honey, honey, that sweetness will come into the mouth. *(unknown)*

40. It is only a mad man that goes to bed with his roof on fire. *(unknown)*

41. Move your neck according to the music. (Ethiopia)

42. Take a woman to bed and she gladly gives her heart. Anger a woman in bed, and she gives you her knife. *(unknown)*

43. Tell me who you love and I will tell you who you are. *(unknown)*

44. The fish that has a fowl as a friend soon sprouts wings. *(unknown)*

45. The man who marries a beautiful woman, and the farmer who grows maize by the roadside, have the same problem. *(unknown)*

46. The surest way to a man's heart is through his stomach. *(unknown)*

47. There are many fish in the sea, but only one rocked my boat. *(unknown)*

48. When the music changes, so does the dance. *(unknown)*

49. When you are lost, do not walk fast. *(unknown)*

50. When you live next to the cemetery, you cannot weep for everyone. *(unknown)*

The Bachelors and the Python (A Central African Folktale)

Once, there were only two unmarried men in a certain African village. All of the other adult men had found suitable partners. Kalemeleme, one of the unmarried men, was thought to be too gentle. He was a loving and kind man, but the women took his kindness for granted because he would not stand up for his own rights. On the other hand, Kinku, the other unmarried man, was so bad-tempered that no one could stand him or his tantrums. The women in the village tended to avoid Kinku. The end result was that the two men were very unhappy.

One early morning when the dew was on the grass, Kalemeleme took his bow and arrows and went hunting in the forest. After hiding in wait, he then shot a grey wild-cat and a brown wild-cat. On his way back to the village, he met Moma, the great rock python, and mightiest snake in the forest. He was about to shoot Moma when the python pleaded, "Gentle one, have mercy on me, for I am stiff with cold. Take me to the river where it is warm."

Touched with pity, Kalemeleme took the great reptile on his shoulders and gave him a lift to the stream. Upon reaching the bank, Kalemeleme allowed Moma to slip gently into the water. In gratitude, Moma lifted his head above the reeds and said to the unmarried man, "Thank you, gentle one. I have seen your loneliness. Throw in your grey wild-cat and your brown wild-cat and take what the water-spirit gives you."

As instructed, Kalemeleme threw his grey wild-cat and his brown wild-cat into the river. Immediately, the water began to ripple and grow redder and redder until beneath the surface there appeared a great, red, open mouth. Kalemeleme then put in his hand and pulled out a gourd. When he took it home and opened it, out stepped the most beautiful girl Kalemeleme had ever seen. The beautiful woman could weave mats, plait baskets, and make pots; she kept the house so neat, and cultivated the garden. The lovely woman from the gourd also prepared the food so carefully and helped her neighbors so willingly that soon Kalemeleme and his beautiful wife were the favorites of the village.

Upon seeing the beautiful wife Kalemeleme had brought home, Kinku asked of his dear friend, "Dear friend, tell me, where did you get your wife?

"The water-spirit gave her to me," Kalemeleme replied.

After telling Kinku what had happened, Kinku jumped and shouted happily, "Well, I want a wife too!" So he took his bow and his arrows and went off into the forest when the sun was boiling hot overhead. After a while, he too killed a grey wild-cat and a brown wild-cat. On his way home, he too met Moma, the mighty python. The great snake was wilting in the heat under a bush. He was about to shoot the snake when Moma pleaded, "Mercy, Kinku. Have mercy on me for I am suffocating with this heat. Take me on your shoulders to the river where it's cool."

"What! Take you, a loathsome reptile?" shouted Kinku, "Find your own way to the river!"

"Very well, come along," said the great python, slowly snaking his way through the undergrowth while Kinku followed a safe distance behind him. When Moma came to the water's edge, he immersed the entire length of his body. With impatience, Kinku waited and waited until the great python, refreshed, lifted his head above the reeds and called out to Kinku. "Kinku, I have seen your loneliness. Now, throw in your grey wild-cat and your brown wild-cat and take what the water-spirit gives you."

With a bit of uncertainty, Kinku threw in his grey wild-cat and his brown wild-cat. At once, just as his friend Kalemeleme had said in his miraculous story, the water began to ripple and became redder and redder, until beneath the surface Kinku saw a huge open mouth. As Kalemeleme had instructed, Kinku put in his hand. He was surprised when he pulled out a pumpkin instead of a gourd, but knowing he would find his wife inside, Kinku staggered home with it.

As Kinku made his way back to his village, the pumpkin became heavier and heavier. At last, he dropped the heavy pumpkin and when it landed on the ground it cracked open and out stepped the ugliest woman he had ever seen. Before Kinku could recover from his shock, the ugly woman boxed him soundly on the ears. She then took him by the nose and snarled, "Come on Kinku, I am your wife." The ugly woman didn't give Kinku the chance to say "no," she pummeled, pulled, biffed, bullied, and blamed him every step of the way. Back at the village, Kinku's ugly wife led him a dog's life. She was as lazy as she was hideous and ordered him about mercilessly. "Kinku, carry the water! Kinku, cut the firewood! Kinku, cultivate the garden! Kinku, cook the meal!" As she did all this, Kinku's ugly wife simply lay about thinking of new ways to abuse her husband. Of course, Kinku complained in the village square, but as a rule no one listened. Who didn't have their own problems and everyone knew not only that home affairs are not talked about on the public square, but also, the path Kinku was walking was the one he made himself.

Something to think about!

Chapter 6 – War and Conflict

The Gentleman of the Jungle (A Kenyan Fable)

Once upon a time an elephant made friends with a man. One day a heavy thunderstorm broke out and the elephant went to his friend, who had a little hut at the edge of the forest, and asked, "My dear good man, will you please let me put just my trunk inside your hut to keep it out of this torrential rain?" The man, believing he had plenty of room for his friend's trunk and himself replied, "Of course my dear friend. Please put your trunk in gently." The elephant thanked his friend, saying that one day he would return the kindness. However, as soon as the elephant put his trunk inside the hut, the head, ears, body and tail followed until the elephant pushed the man out in the torrential rain. As the elephant lay down comfortably inside his friend's hut, he said to the man, "My dear good friend, your skin is harder than mine, and besides, there is not enough room for both of us."

The man, seeing that he had been tricked, started to grumble so loud he woke up the other animals. Also awakened from his nap was Lion, who roared, "Don't you know that I am the King of the jungle! How dare anyone disturb the peace of my kingdom?" On hearing the lion, elephant, who was one of the high ministers in the jungle kingdom, replied in a soothing voice, "My Lord, I truly apologize, but man and I are having a little dispute over this hut, which you can clearly see that I am occupying." Butting in, fearing the lion would be swayed by the elephant's one-sided story, the man objected, arguing that the sly elephant pushed him out of his own hut. Growling fiercely, since the lion wanted to have peace and tranquility in his kingdom, he ordered everyone back to their homes and to reassemble in court the next morning.

"But what of my hut?" complained the man, to which the lion replied, "You have tough skin, sleep out under the stars tonight." Without another word, all the animals bedded down for the night, as well as man himself.

That night, the man was forced to sleep under a large acacia tree far away from his house. In the morning, when he appeared in court, all the other animals had already assembled. The man was very pleased, and when ordered to tell his story, he did so. The man thought he was well on his way to getting his home back, as the animals who had assembled were nodding with his every word.

But then, the elephant told a much more elaborate and believable story. He explained how foolish it sounded for him to be afraid of just his trunk getting wet. The man could see the jurors nodding to the elephant's story as they had his. The elephant then explained how he had been promised payment for shoring up the man's house and even fixing a leak in the ceiling. It was only after the man refused to pay that fair compensation gave me permission to occupy the house.

"Seems plausible," Lion roared softly as if seriously pondering his good friend's story, "but it is not for me alone to decide." The lion then ordered the members of the jury, Mr. Rhinoceros; Mr. Buffalo; Mr. Alligator; The Honorable Mr. Fox, and Mr. Leopard, to deliberate upon the matter and deliver a verdict. "But, your honor," the man objected, "are there no men on the jury that may possibly see things as I do?" To this, the lion growled in anger. "Do you dare challenge my royal wisdom, not to mention the honor of the people of this court?" The man, fearing for his safety, decided it was best to apologize and hope for the best. "I met no disrespect," he humbly spoke. "I will respect and honor the decision of such a wise king and the honorable jury." To this the lion roared with content, "Good, now be patient. If you have spoken truthfully, you will have your hut back."

Well, after fifteen minutes of discussion, Mrs. Rhinoceros, who was head of the jury, approached the lion and spoke. 'Gentlemen of the jungle, after hearing both sides of the story, we have come to a conclusion. It was made clear to all with ears enough to listen, that the man sought only to confiscate what was not ever his in the first place. Furthermore, being a lazy sort, he invited Mr. Elephant in to fix-up his meager dwelling and then reneged on the payment. Of course, work done is work that should be paid for, and since Mr. Man had never intended to pay Mr. Elephant for his work, it was only fair that his hut be forfeited in return."

"Then, it is settled," growled the lion, "my dear and honorable friend, Mr. Elephant shall continue to rightfully live in the man's house." Baring his sharp canines at the man, lion then inquired whether he had anything to say." The man, fearing deciding it was safer to keep his opinions to himself, politely shook his head and left the court.

Picking up his belongings, the man waved farewell to the few friends who wished him well, but dare not object in his favor, and went on his way. It was not long before he found a suitable place to build another hut. But no sooner had he built this hut, Mr. Rhinoceros lowered his horn and charged in. "Out!" he ordered the man, pushing him steadily out the door. Days later, the rhinoceros and the man had their day in court. To the man's chagrin, he found himself facing the same jury as before. This time Mr. Buffalo was head juror, with Mr. Leopard, Mr. Hyena, Mr. Fox, and Mr. Elephant were waiting to hear his story. As it had been before, the animals ruled against the man, and he was sent in search of yet another place to build a house.

Insistent, the man traveled even farther away this time and built an even better house. For a time he had peace and even had some of the animals in the jury over for polite conversation. Then, one day he came home and found Mr. Fox and Mr. Leopard stretched out in his lawn chair. When he tried to enter his house the two animals stood on all four legs and bared their sharp teeth at him. "We," they said in unison, "have been laying here for days in this abandoned house. You cannot just claim it." Then, laughing, leopard suggested the man take them to court, and let a jury decide.

Well, the man being no fool, again packed up his belongings, which Mr. Leopard and Mr. Fox had tossed into the courtyard, and sulked off. After having traveled a great distance he came upon a clearing where he began building the best house of all. It was a large house, with a high ceiling, wide walkways, an indoor swimming pool, and all the amenities a fine house could have. From afar, Mr. Elephant and Mr. Giraffe could see the splendor. Oh, what a beautiful, gleaming house it was all the animals of the jungle agreed. Then, while the man went off, probably to fish in nearby lake, Mr. Elephant and Mr. Rhinoceros, as well as Mr. Wolf, Mr. Lion, and Mr. Fox came and took possession of the house. So busy were they enjoying their new home that not a one noticed the man nailing all the doors and windows shut. They did not notice the fire either, that is not until it was too late. Though the house had been so very beautiful, it had served its purpose with all of the man's so-called friends trapped inside never to be seen again. Then, the man went off singing to himself, "Peace is costly, but it's worth the expense."

The original author of this story is Jomo Kenyatta, an African nationalist and first Prime Minister of Kenya (1963). He is also the author of Facing Mount Kenya, an anthropological study of the Kikuyu tribe of Kenya, from which he was born.

Something to think about!

African Proverbs

1. To punch with a strong fist, you need to turn over your hand. (Angola)

2. The ruin of a nation begins in the homes of its people. (*Ashanti*)

3. Until the lion has his or her own storyteller, the hunter will always have the best part of the story. (*Benin, Ghana, and Togo*)

4. The chicken is never declared innocent in the court of hawks. (*Ghana*)

5. Though the lion and the antelope happen to live in the same forest, the antelope still has time to grow up. (*Ghana*)

6. War is not porridge. (*Kenya*)

7. We should put out fire while it is still small. (*Kenya*)

8. An eye that you treat is the one that turns against you. (*Kenya, Tanzania*)

9. The tree will never forget the axe that cut it, but how soon the axe forgets. (*Mozambique, Zimbabwe, Zambia*)

10. A king's child is a slave elsewhere. (*Mozambique, Zimbabwe, Zambia*)

11. What forgets is the axe, but the tree that has been axed will never forget. (*Mozambique, Zimbabwe, Zambia*)

12. A cockroach knows how to sing and dance, but it is the hen that prevents it from performing its art during the day. (*Nigeria*)

13. The frog does not run in the daytime for nothing. (*Nigeria*)

14. If a toad jumps around in the daytime, it is either chasing something or something is chasing it. (*Nigeria*)

15. When the bush is on fire, the antelope ceases to fear the hunter's bullet. (*Nigeria*)

16. When the elephants fight it is the grass that suffers. (*Nigeria*)

17. The house-roof fights with the rain, but he who is sheltered ignores it. (*Senegal*)

18. Let rats shoot arrows at each other. (*Sudan*)

19. Great fires erupt from tiny sparks. (*Sudan*)

20. Like vomit and shit under your feet, the rumor monger spreads scandal. (*Tanzania, Mozambique*)

21. A close friend can become a close enemy. (Ethiopia)

22. A little subtleness is better than a lot of force. (*unknown*)

23. He that digs up a grave for his enemy, may be digging it for himself. (*unknown*)

24. If you are in hiding, don't light a fire. (*unknown*)

25. A weapon which you don't have in your hand won't kill a snake. (*unknown*)

26. An intelligent enemy is better than a stupid friend. (*unknown*)

27. Ashes fly back into the face of him who throws them. (*unknown*)

28. Do not step on the dog's tail and he will not bite you. (*unknown*)

29. Great towns grow with peace but not by killing and intimidation. *(unknown)*

30. He who has done evil, expects evil. *(unknown)*

31. If an enemy learns your dance, he/she dances it the crooked way. *(unknown)*

32. If you want a man to hate you then make him think. *(unknown)*

33. Peace is costly but it is worth the expense. *(unknown)*

34. Peace-talk comes after war. *(unknown)*

35. To engage in conflict, one does not bring a knife that cuts – but a needle that sews. *(unknown)*

36. When a king has good counselors, his reign is peaceful. *(unknown)*

37. It is best to let the stew cool before sipping of it. *(unknown)*

38. When the biggest lion meets the biggest buffalo, even if the lion kills the buffalo, he will never eat it. *(unknown)*

39. When the cock is drunk he forgets about the hawk. *(Ghana)*

40. Whether the knife falls on the melon or the melon on the knife, the melon suffers. *(unknown)*

41. Wood already touched by fire is not hard to set alight. *(unknown)*

42. One does not fight to save another person's head only to have a kite carry one's own away. *(Yoruba)*

43. Harsh world, this world. *(Zulu)*

44. A slave has no choice. *(Kenya)*

45. One should never rub bottoms with a porcupine. *(Akan)*

46. It is better to be the cub of a live jackal than of a dead lion. (Ethiopia)

47. The one who is mistaken is the one who does nothing. *(Ethiopia)*

48. Because a man has injured your goat, do not go out and kill his bull. *(Kenya)*

49. Malice drinketh its own poison. *(Egypt)*

50. A leader does not wish for war. *(Kenya)*

Only the Cook Knows What's in the Stew (Aesop's Fable)

It was growing cold as winter was approaching, and Mother and Father Porcupine along with their child was looking for a home. When they did find a desirable burrow in the ground, it was occupied by the Mole family. "Would you mind if we shared your home for the winter?" Mother and Father Porcupine asked Mother and Father Mole. Always willing to help out a friend, the Moles consented, but only for a day or two. Seemingly gracious, the Porcupine family waddled in.

To their displeasure, weeks went by and the Porcupine family appeared to have no intention of moving out to find their own burrow. The burrow was small to begin with, in addition, every time the moles moved around they were stung by the sharp quills of the porcupines. The moles somehow endured the discomfort until the end of winter. When the first sign of spring came, Mother and Father Mole asked the visiting Porcupine family to leave. "Oh no!" said the porcupines. "This place suits us very well. If you're not happy, then YOU should leave!"

Mother and Father Mole explained how cramped their living quarters had become and showed their visitors the scratches on their once beautiful and shiny fur coats. "Tsk, tsk," replied Mother and Father Porcupine, "that is your own doing. You knew we had sharp quills when you invited us to stay." Then, settling back in their chair, Mother and Father Porcupine inquired when dinner was to be served, being that Mother Mole was an excellent cook.

The next day, Father Mole got up, put on his work clothes and readied himself to go out in the field to harvest yams. "Come along," he said to their child, "we will bring back momma the sweetest yams." Then, Father Mole tried to kiss Mother Mole, but before their lips could even touch, they winced in pain from being stuck by a porcupine quill. "Ouch!" they all cried. "We must do something about our unwelcomed guests," complained Father Mole. "Yes," cried Baby Mole, pulling out a sharp needle. "Today, I will," winced Mother Mole, pulling a quill from her skin. "Double ouch!"

After getting her kisses and hugs, Mother Mole set about cooking a large pot of sweet, smelling stew. The porcupine family, a lazy bunch, did not leave their burrow at all, and it was such a fine, summer day. All the porcupine family did, father, mother, and child, was laze around with their bellies grumbling in anticipation of getting at the awfully sweet smelling stew Mother Mole was making. While the stew was cooking, Mother Mole swept up needles and tided up around the porcupine family. It was nothing for Mother Mole to keep her burrow clean, but this time she feigned she was tired and needed to go out for some fresh air. "Mother Porcupine," she called as she was leaving, "I am going out for just a little while. I think I will also visit Mother Rabbit. Would you like to come?"

Having long overstayed their welcome, Mother Porcupine feared a little trickery was afoot. "Oh, no thank you," Mother Porcupine answered. "I am rather tired today. While you are out I will watch to keep your sweet smelling stew from burning."

"Oh, thank you," Mother Mole called down into the burrow, indeed the sun on her fur felt so very good. "Please come and get me when it is ready so that I may add a few more of my special herbs and spices to it to make it just right."

"Oh, I will," promised Mother Porcupine, having no such intent. "As soon as it is done, I will send Baby Porcupine out to get you. You can be sure of that."

Of course, Mother Mole knew no such thing was going to happen. In fact, no sooner had she disappeared from sight, she could hear Mother Porcupine calling her husband and child over to her pot of stew. With a smile on her face, Mother Mole went right on over to her friend Mother Rabbit and enjoyed the rest of the day. While Mother Mole was at Mother Rabbit's house, and Father and Baby Mole was out harvesting the sweetest of yams, the greedy porcupine family sat around the Mole's small table eating up all of stew. When the pot was empty, with not even a drop left for the Mole family, the Porcupine family waddled off into their respective corners and fell fast asleep.

When Mother Porcupine returned from visiting Mother Rabbit, she noticed that her pot was empty and the porcupine family was lying on their bloated sides. "Oh, Mother Mole," Mother Porcupine cried out in pain, "you have put too much shitto (hot pepper sauce) in the stew. I don't think you need a pinch more." Father Mole cried out as well, noticing his sharp quills starting to fall off, "Oh, Mother Mole, the curry rice is too spicy! It needs not one more sprinkle of pepper." Finally, Baby Porcupine whimpered, "Oh, Mother Mole, the stew is too sweet. I am so sick. Please, not another spoonful of honey!"

Mother Mole's pot of stew had been the greedy porcupines undoing. Having overstayed their welcome, the porcupine family rolled about the floor with severe stomach pains. "Ay," cried out Mother Porcupine one last time, "family, I think we have been poisoned. I have never tasted such koobi (salted tilapia) before. It has all of our stomachs on fire."

Looking into the emptiness of her once full pot of stew, Mother Mole let out a devious laugh, "Oh, my dearest porcupine friend, would I do such a thing as that?"

"Yes, I think you would," grunted Mother Porcupine. "Why else would I have this fat and bloated body?" Father Porcupine grumbled in agreement, "Why else would my beautiful quills be falling off?" Finally, Baby Porcupine's last squealed, "Mommy, let's go home. I am so sick."

Unfortunately, just as there was not a drop of the poisoned stew left, there was not an ounce of sympathy for Mother

Porcupine, her husband, nor her child. "I have no idea what you are talking about," replied Mother Mole. "Perhaps you are gravely sick because you emptied the entire pot of my stew into your bellies, leaving not an ounce for me, my husband, nor my child. Perhaps it is because I was not sent for as promised when my stew was ready. Perhaps it is because you are having stomach pains and your sharp needles are falling off your fat bellies because all of you are feeling guilty for overstaying your welcome."

By the time Mother Mole had finished listing all the reasons for the porcupine family's demise, her little burrow was full of silence. The entire porcupine family had succumbed to the stew Mother Mole had made especially for them; knowing they would eat every bit of it without consideration for her and her family. "Oh, what a wonderful place," she began singing, washing out the pot to start a fresh and hardy stew that would be so delicious with the sweet yams Father and Baby Mole were bringing home. "Oh you prickly devils, how our humble abode suited you well. Now and forever more, my most undesirable friends, the last of my stew have you smelled."

That night, after having enjoyed Mother Mole's delicious yam stew, and after Baby Mole had read to them from his favorite book of Anansi's Tales, Mother and Father Mole lay lovingly in each other's arms. "Before one eats, one should examine the meat," whispered Father Mole. "True," replied his wife, "but remember this, my husband, only the cook knows what's in the pot."

Something to think about!

War and Conflict

Chapter 7 – Wealth, Money, Greed, and Thieves

Abu Nuwasi Sells His House (A Kenyan Folktale)

Abu Nuwasi was a successful and honest merchant. After many years of trading his goods at the market he had saved up enough money to build a house. When the house was finished it had many rooms and two floors. After moving in and seeing the house was really too big for him, he decided to sell the top floor to a banker.

As he had always done, Abu Nuwasi continued to be honest with his trading at the market and just as profitable. After a number of years went by, he decided he would move to a new village. Having made more than enough money, and with no prospects in his current village, he decided he would move to another town to find a wife and raise a family. So, having made up his mind about leaving, he approached the banker living on the top floor of his house. Hoping for an honest and fair price, Abu Nuwasi offered the first floor to the banker. Knowing that the banker was even richer than himself, Abu Nuwasi had no intentions on selling his half of the house for one less than his house was worth, nor of course, one penny more either.

When approached, the banker contemplated the fair offer but then declined. See, the banker was really a greedy and devious sort. He indeed needed more room for his business was growing. Having heard rumors that Abu Nuwasi wanting to move to another town, the dishonest banker refused to loan the money to anyone wanted to buy Abu Nuwasi's half of the house. The dishonest banker was hoping that Abu Nuwasi would get frustrated and simply leave him the entire house for free.

Well, Abu Nuwasi was not only an honest merchant; he was a smart merchant as well. When it became apparent to him what the unscrupulous banker was doing he went into town and gathered up a dozen workers, who followed him home with their hammers, shovels, axes and other tools. Abu Nuwasi then went upstairs to talk to the greedy and dishonest banker one more time. "I have come to inform you that since you are not interested in buying my half of the house, nor are you allowing anyone else to do so, I have hired some workers to help me destroy my half of my home. Take a look outside your window," he suggested. Hearing the clamor outside his window, the greedy and dishonest banker looked down and saw a dozen strong men anxious for work. "Of course," Abu

Nuwasi said with a straight and honest face, "you can remain in your half as they will only destroy my bottom half."

Needless to say, the greedy banker quickly changed his mind and decided to purchase the lower half of the house from Abu Nuwasi. The price he paid however was even more than the Abu Nuwasi's original offer. The price now tripled, one third for the house itself, an additional third for the banker's deceitful and greed, and a final third to pay the dozen workers who had followed him home with their hammers, shovels, axes and other tools with the promise of work.

Something to think about!

African Proverbs

1. Money is sharper than the sword. (*Ghana*)
2. One cannot both feast and become rich. (*Ghana*)
3. The poor man and the rich man do not play together. (*Ghana*)
4. Knowledge is better than riches. (*Cameroon, Nigeria*)
5. The person who has eaten and satisfied himself or herself does not care for the one who is hungry. (*Cameroon, Nigeria*)
6. A debt is not a loss once one knows the debtor. (*Democratic Republic of Congo*)

7. The one who eats has tasted the hardship of labor. (*Democratic Republic of Congo*)

8. There is no one who became rich because he broke a holiday; no one became fat because he broke a fast. (Ethiopia)

9. Along with your struggles, count your blessing. (*Ghana*)

10. If you see a man going to his farm in kente cloth, don't jump into conclusion that he is very rich. (*Ghana*)

11. The one who fetches the water is the one who is likely to break the pot. (*Ghana*)

12. The person who tends to ingratiate himself to his father without involving others never inherits the father's property. (*Kenya*)

13. A thieving dog knows itself. (*Kenya*)

14. Use of brains begets wealth. (*Kenya*)

15. The only value a slave has is the one his master gives him. (*Liberia*)

16. It's better to give than to receive. (*Madagascar*)

17. The one never satisfied goes to bed with an empty stomach, empty pockets. (*Malawi, Tanzania, Zimbabwe*)

18. The hyena chasing two antelopes at the same time will go to bed hungry. (*Mali*)

19. He who loves money must labor. (*Mauritana*)

20. One cannot count on riches. Somalia. (*Somalia*)

21. Poverty is slavery. (*Somalia*)

22. The person who has a light knee can survive longer. (*Sudan*)

23. He who plays the pipe calls for the tune. (*Twi*)

24. With wealth one wins a woman. Uganda. (*Uganda*)

25. Being well dressed does not prevent one from being poor. (*unknown*)

26. Do not measure the timbers for your house in the forest. (*unknown*)

27. Do not say the first thing that comes to your mind. (*unknown*)

28. Don't take another mouthful before you have swallowed what is in your mouth. (*unknown*)

29. Hunger is felt by both the slave and the king. (*unknown*)

30. If the palm of the hand itches it signifies the coming of great luck. (*unknown*)

31. Knowledge is like a garden: if it is not cultivated, it cannot be harvested. (*unknown*)

32. Poverty is not lack of money, but it is lack of knowledge and ability. (*unknown*)

33. The thief will cry foul when his goods are stolen. (*unknown*)

34. It is the calm and silent water that drowns a man. (*unknown*)

35. Better a bird in hand then two in the bush. (*unknown*)

36. The drunkard's money is being consumed by palm-wine trapper. (*unknown*)

37. God made man, man made money but money corrupts man. *(unknown)*

38. Gradually but continuously can wealth be demolished. *(unknown)*

39. He who plays with chickens soils his hands with chicken's droppings. (unknown)

40. If you run after two hares you will catch neither. (unknown)

41. If you want to swallow a mango seed, you first of all calculate the diameter of your anus. *(unknown)*

42. It is the sack of chickens that draws the hyenas out. *(unknown)*

43. Join me in a meal is not join me in a work. *(unknown)*

44. Looking at a king's mouth one would never think he sucked his mother's breast. *(unknown)*

45. No one drinks hot pepper soup in a hurry. *(unknown)*

46. Poverty is madness. *(unknown)*

47. The stomach does not allow the feet to rest. *(unknown)*

48. A crime eats its own child. *(South Africa)*

49. Success does not come the way of fools. *(unknown)*

50. If you are rich, you are out of many problems, yet you formulate many lies. *(Tanzania)*

Wealth, Money, Greed, and Thieves

The Rabbit Who Stole the Elephant's Dinner

(A Central African Tale)

One day while Kalulu the rabbit was watching the children of Soko the monkey playing in the trees, he saw one monkey reach out his tail and catch the other around the neck and hold him helplessly in mid-air. Only after much begging and pleading did the monkey let the other go, after which the two monkeys continued with their play. Kalulu, a jovial trickster, thought it was a splendid way to catch other animals and watch in merriment as they tried to escape. Though he had long ears, Kalulu had only a bushy tail, so he devised another way to carry out his plan. Shortly thereafter, a number of animals were being caught in a similar fashion as they were going about their merry way in the forest. Though none were hurt, and all thought it was only an accident, Kalulu found experimenting with his noose to be such great fun.

Well, one day, Polo the elephant decided that it was time for a new village. Being that he was king of the animals, he called every living thing in the forest to come and help build the village. All came as were called, except of course, Kalulu. See, not only was Kalulu not prone to working anyway, he had also caught a whiff of the delicious beans Polo's wives were cooking to serve the worker when they retired for the day. When Polo's wives were not looking, because who would dare steal the king's beans, Kalulu came out of the bushes and ate them all up. When Polo the elephant returned home with the other tired and hungry animals, he was furious to find not a bean in the pot. Whoever could have taken all of their dinner he wondered?

The next day Polo told the lion to lie in wait nearby. The lion's orders were to pounce upon the thief once the brave soul appeared. Now, all this time Kalulu was hiding in the bushes and so he spent that night twisting a big noose which he hid under leaves and branches close to the cooking pots. As usual, the next morning when the Polo and the other animals had gone to work on the new village, Kalulu strolled out into the open and began to eat Polo's beans. All along he knew where the lion was hiding. When he finished his meal, Kalulu ran off, and as expected, Ntambo the lion leapt out in hot pursuit. Kalulu was a fast runner, but no match for Ntambo, who one day fancied to be king himself. Just as Ntambo was about to close his claws around Kalulu's neck, the lion stepped right into the noose that had been laid as a trap. As the Lion swung in the air, wriggling and squirming, Kalulu continued on holding his side with uncontained laughter. Later that evening, when the animals returned, Ntambo was set free. Too ashamed to admit he had been fooled by a Kalulu, a little rabbit, Ntambo simply said that some unknown animal had ensnared him.

The next day Polo, the elephant, gave Mbo the buffalo, the chore of watch the beans, but again Kalulu had set a great noose between two palm trees. As had occurred the previous day, when Kalulu had finished his meal of the chief's beans and was strolling away, the Mbo the buffalo burst out into the opening and was on his hills. Kalulu could have easily outrun Mbo, but in merriment he ran between the two palm trees. When Mbo followed, hoping to ensnare Kululu with his horns, the huge buffalo was caught by the noose. Up, up and away, Mbo began to swing, wriggle and squirmed as Kululu laughed till his side hurt. When the animals returned that evening, they set him loose as they had Ntambo the lion. As was the lion, Mbo was so ashamed that he has been outwitted by a small rabbit, his only remark was that there must be some misdoer dwelling among them. Days later, the leopard, the lynx, the wart-hog and the hunting dog were all fooled in the same way, and still Kalulu the rabbit stole Polo's daily bowl of beans.

At last, Nkuvu the tortoise, wiser than even Kalulu, went privately to King Polo the elephant. "If your wives will smear me with salt and put me into your dinner of beans tomorrow, I will catch the thief," he assured. Agreeing, that is exactly what happened and the next day Nkuvu was secretly smeared with salt and hidden in the beans.

Having outsmarted many an animal, and loving the idea of no work and all play, Kalulu determined to get his dinner without working for it. He had overheard that warthog would be his next victim. This would be the easiest day of all he thought, knowing exactly where the overweight beast was sleeping. So, having set his noose, Kalulu sauntered up to the cooking pots when all the animals had left to work on the new village and began eating. Smacking his lips and wiggling his long rabbit ears, the rabbit thought the beans were even more delicious than usual. Then, just as he was about to finish, Nkuvu the tortoise bit down onto Kalulu's foot. "Ouch!" the rabbit screamed, pleading, threatened and even offering bribes to the turtle. It was all to no purpose.

When the sun was low in the horizon, Polo and the other animals came back to the village expecting a hearty meal of beans. Nkuvu having said nothing, had simply held on to Kalulu's foot until they had all returned. Upon seeing Nkuvu holding on tightly to Kalulu, at once they all knew who the thief really was, and they determined to pay him back exactly as he had treated them. For six days he had to go without any dinner, and every day they went off to work leaving Kalulu tied by a noose and hanging from a tree. Everyday Kalulu had to endure not just the heat, but the torments of the monkeys who he had gotten the idea from. On the seventh day, Kalulu was so thin that the animals took pity on him and let him go. They warned him however, that it was better to work for his food than to steal it, and though a thief may escape for a time, one day he is surely to be caught.

Something to think about!

Chapter 8 – Cowards, Pride, and Fools

Jackal, Dove, and Heron

Jackal, it is said, came once to Dove, who lived on the top of a rock, and said, "Give me one of your little ones."

Dove answered, "I shall not do anything of the kind."

Jackal then said, "Give me it at once, otherwise, I shall fly up to you."

Afraid, Dove threw one of her little one down to Jackal. The next day, Jackal came back and demanded another little one. Again, torn with fright, Dove gave it to him. Now, after Jackal had gone, Heron came up to see her friend. Dove, "why do you cry?" she asked.

Dove answered, "Jackal has taken away my little ones; that is why I am always crying."

Curious, Heron asked her friend how in the world Jackal could do such a thing, for he knew the sly animal could not climb high up in the tree where Dove had her nest. "When he asked me at first," whimpered Dove, "I refused. But then Jackal said he would fly up here and eat all of my babies. Therefore, sister, I threw them down as he requested."

"Oh sister, are you such a fool to give your babies to Jackal. That moron cannot fly? How stupid of you. I shall never be so dumb." Then, Heron left her good friend Dove and to go bathing in a nearby lake.

Shortly after Heron left Dove, Jackal came along as he had been doing for the past two days. "Dove," he called up, "give me a little one." Taking Heron's advice, Dove refused. "Heron," she sang. "I am no fool. Heron told me that you have no wings to fly. So, you will have no more of my babies."

Furious, Jackal turned stomped of into the brush with his belly grumbling. Having grown soft for not having to hunt, every animal he chased easily eluded him. Upon coming to a lake to quench his thirst from all the running he had been doing, Jackal saw elegant Heron and called for her to come over. Not nearly as foolish as her good friend, Dove, Heron came only to the edge of the water. "What do you want, Jackal?" she asked cautiously, standing on the bank.

"Sister Heron," Jackal answered, "when the wind comes from the side, how do you stand?"

Answering, Heron turned her neck towards Jackal and said, "I stand by bending my neck on one side like this." Then Heron demonstrated by bending her neck slightly to one side.

"Interesting," barked Jackal. "Well then, when a storm comes and when it rains, how do you stand?"

"I stand like this," Heron said, eager to demonstrate by standing on one leg.

"That is just as interesting," Jackal smiled. "And so, how do you eat. Can you even do such a thing?"

"Oh, absolutely," Heron boasted. "I just bend my neck down like so, right into the water."

In a flash, Jackal leaped upon Heron and broke her neck in the middle. Because he had not had any of Dove's baby chicks that day, his bite was weak and Heron was able to wiggle her neck free. Since that day however, herons' neck have been bent. When Dove saw her friend, "Girlfriend," she flapped, "just as you knew that Jackal couldn't fly, you should have known his character is like smoke. It cannot be hidden."

Cowards, Pride, and Fools

Something to think about!

African Proverbs

1. His opinions are like water in the bottom of a canoe, going from side to side. (*Nigeria*)
2. It is foolhardy to climb two trees at once just because one has two feet. (Ethiopia)
3. The good looks of a moron do not stay that way for long. (Ethiopia)
4. The haughty blind person picks a fight with his guide. (Ethiopia)
5. What can a stick do when I have already swallowed the gong? (*Uganda*)
6. He is a fool whose sheep runs away twice. (*Ghana*)
7. It is a fool who rejoices when his neighbor is in trouble. (*Ghana*)
8. Fine clothes may disguise a fool, but silly words will always strip him bare. (*unknown*)
9. The pigeon is overlooked for the peacock. (*Ghana*)
10. Whenever you are short of funds, even a fool will advise you. (*Ghana*)
11. Where error gets to, correction cannot reach. (*Ghana*)
12. He who eats with devil use to eat with long spoon. (*Igbo*)

13. To be praised is to be lost. (*Kenya*)

14. A fool has many days. (*Kenya*)

15. The eye is a coward. (*Kenya*)

16. There is no hyena without a friend. (*Kenya*)

17. Water cannot be forced uphill. (*Kenya*)

18. When a long teeth man is dying you say he is laughing. (*Liberia*)

19. Mr. Run-to-get-warm left the fire as it was beginning to blaze. (*Malawi, Tanzania, Zimbabwe*)

20. He flees from the roaring lion to the crouching lion. (*Sechuana*)

21. Do not tell the man carrying you that he stinks. (*Sierra Leone*)

22. The camel does not see the bend in its neck. (*Sudan [North Africa]*)

23. I pointed out to you the stars (the moon) and all you saw was the tip of my finger. (*Tanzania, Mozambique*)

24. Swallow saliva before you cross a one log bridge. (*Tanzania, Mozambique*)

25. A stubborn person sails in a clay boat. (*Tanzania*)

26. A monkey left behind laughs at the others tail. (*Uganda*)

27. The person who has not traveled widely thinks his or her mother is the only cook. (*Uganda*)

28. A fool and water will go the way they are diverted. (Ethiopia)

29. A fool looks for dung where the cow never browsed. *(unknown)*

30. A fool will pair an ox with an elephant. *(unknown)*

31. A proud heart can survive a general failure because such a failure does not prick its pride. *(unknown)*

32. Too modest of a man goes hungry. (Ethiopia)

33. After a foolish deed comes remorse. *(unknown)*

34. By the time the fool has learned the game, the players have dispersed. *(unknown)*

35. Even over cold pudding, the coward says, it will burn my mouth. *(unknown)*

36. He who forgives ends the argument. *(unknown)*

37. He who hunts two rats, catches none. *(unknown)*

38. He who talks incessantly talks nonsense. *(unknown)*

39. It is no shame at all to work for money. *(Ghana)*

40. The fool who wrestles with another fool is always bested twice; the first by the fool in him, and the second by the other fool. *(unknown)*

41. A baby will fall into a crocodile's mouth, a fool will open the crocodile's mouth, a hunter will kill the crocodile, and a wife will cook it. *(unknown)*

42. A blind wise man may lead a fool, but a blind fool is ridiculed by children. *(unknown)*

43. A fool is always right in his own eyes– no wonder he is a fool. *(unknown)*

44. A fool may chance to put something into a wise man's head. *(unknown)*

45. A good thing sells itself, a bad one advertises itself. *(unknown)*

46. A head with no sense is burdening the neck. *(unknown)*

47. A stubborn chicken learns it lesson in a hot pot of soup. *(unknown)*

48. He who is born a fool is never cured. *(unknown)*

49. He who wrestles with a gorilla will find his back dusty. *(unknown)*

50. If you hear a mad man talking, wait for a minute you will hear what makes people think he is mad. *(unknown)*

The Lion and the Mouse (A Nigerian Folktale)

One day Lion, who was the king of all animals and who feared nothing, was asleep. As he slept, Mouse crawled on top of him and started playing. While Mouse played, lion dreamed that something was playing on his side. When he slowly opened his eyes and saw Mouse, in an instant he had the miniature animal in his claws. Poor Mouse cried, "Great one, will you not let me go? You know I may be able to do something for you some day." Laughing, Lion said, "A little thing like you, what could you do for me?" Whether it was because Lion had no appetite for such a small morsel, felt no threat from Mouse, or just had a kind heart that day, in any regard he let Mouse go. Trembling, Mouse thanked Lion even as he hurried away to hide himself in a hole in the ground.

Many days passed and Lion, all but forgotten about his encounter with Mouse, was off hunting in the high grass. Suddenly, having found himself ensnared in a trap, Lion was unable to move. At first he felt sure that he could free himself, but the harder he pulled the tighter the rope wound around him. With all his might, Lion, the king of beasts, could not break free. It was then, knowing his days were numbered, did the king of animals begin to cry.

Well, Mouse, whose hearing was even keener than Lion's, heard the king of beast whimpering. Emerging from his hole in the ground, Mouse decided to find out what could be wrong with his great and mighty friend. Climbing up on a branch, when he found Lion entangled in ropes, he asked the mighty, yet said to the Lion,

"Don't fret, allow me to let you lose?" When Lion heard his squeaky friend, he grew even more grave. "Oh my dear little friend, I would like that so much, but you are such a little thing. Is it even possible?" With a snicker, Mouse began to nibble and gnaw at the strong rope. In no time at all he had gnawed through it and set Lion free.

Stretching his mighty limbs, the lion looked down upon his little friend, Mouse, with as much surprise as he was thankful. Lion had never imagined that such a little mouse could do anything for him, the king of animals. Amazed that Mouse could save him from death, Lion said, "Had it not been for you, I would have certainly met death at the hands of the owner of the trap. Thank you my little friend." Mouse bowed, shook lion's huge paw, and then squeaked, "You are welcome. One good turn deserves another. Now let's get out of here before we both become dinner."

Something to think about!

Chapter 9 – Fear and Faith

Fear and Faith

The Lost Messages (An Adaptation)

Once, there was a conference of sorts. There was Red-ant,
Rice-ant, Black-ant, Wagtail-ant, Gray-ant, Shining-ant, and many
other varieties of ants. When all the varieties of ants started talking,
their discussion was a true babble of diversity that amounted to
nothing. Some ants thought they should all go into a small hole in
the ground, and live while another group wanted to have a large
and strong dwelling built on the ground where nobody could enter
but an ant. Still another group of ants wanted to dwell in trees, so
as to get rid of Anteater, entirely forgetting about the birds who
loved to feast on them. Yet another group of ants seemed inclined
to have wings and fly, thinking they could out fly the birds. With
so many dissenting opinions, the ant deliberation amounted to
nothing, and at the end of the conference, each party resolved to
go to work in its own way.

As they dispersed, there was great unity among individual ant,
but none amongst the collective. Some even decided to choose a

king to lead them while others thought it wise to choose a queen. Every variety of ant labored in their own way and none thought to form together to protect themselves against Centipede and Jayhawk, Sloth, Lizard, and Anteater. So, the Red-ants built their house on the ground and lived under it. Anteater, of course, leveled the days of precious labor in a minute. The Rice-ants lived under the ground, and with them it went no better. For whenever they came out, Sloth visited them and had a delicious meal of them. The Wagtail-ants fled to the trees, but there awaited Centipede, ready to gobble them up. The Gray-ants had intended to save themselves from extermination by taking flight, but this also availed them nothing. As soon as they showed themselves, Lizard, with his flicking tongue, and Jayhawk who was speedy in flight, had no problems catching and dining on them.

Well, it came to pass, the Insect-king heard of the ants' troubles and knowing the calamitous outcome if they continued on with their disunity, called upon his seven messenger beetles. To each, he whispered a secret message. To Wild Potato Beetle, whose name was Umoja, was told to deliver this message, "that success starts with Unity. Pull together, be open to the positive influence of other, and remember, it is easier to chop down a tree with an ex then break in half a bunch of branches. Go!"

On the second day, Insect-king sent for Rhino Beetle, whose secret name was Kujichagulia. "Have Self-Determination in who you are," he whispered to the second beetle. "Create for yourselves, and speak for yourselves, but remember to have respect for yourselves. Now Go!"

On the third day, Insect-king called Monkey Beetle to him. Monkey Beetle's secret name was Ujima and his message was, "Build and maintain communities with Collective Work and Responsibility. Tell them to go about solving problems and creating opportunities, together. Go!"

When the fourth day arrived, Insect-king sent for Goliath Beetle, whose secret name was Ujamaa. "Ujamaa," Insect-king whispered. "Deliver the message of Cooperative Economics to the ants. Tell them that within your holes and mounds, and trees, and under roots and tall grass," he instructed, "tell ants to build and maintain your own stores, shops, and other marketplaces. Let your dollar circulate at least twelve times before it goes out of your villages. Hurry now, go!" he said to Goliath Beetle.

The next day was the fifth day. "Come," Insect-king called to the Dung Beetle, and in the beetle's ear he whispered, "Nia," which was Dung Beetle's secret name, "tell them to have Purpose. Know that as ants you have a tradition of greatness. Be responsible to those who have come before you. Remember your ancestors and blaze a path for those who will follow. Do not be dissuade because you are small, be determined in your purpose. Now go Nia, deliver my message."

On the sixth day, Insect-king called upon Jewel Beetle, who secret name, Kuumba, King-ant like to draw out as he spoke it. "Kuumbaaaahhhhh," Insect-king whispered, almost as if singing, "Tell the all the many factions and varieties of ants to have Creativity. Kuumbaaahhhh," he whispered a second time, "tell them to always do as much as they can, in the way they can, with what they can, and to maintain the beauty, benefit and purpose of their communities. Now go and deliver this message!" he instructed.

Finally, on the seventh day, after Insect-king had sent the messages of Unity, Self-Determination, Collective work and responsibility, Collective economics, Purpose, and Creativity, he called upon Scarab Beetle to deliver his final, secret message. To Scarab Beetle he whispered with urgent appeal, "Deliver to the ants your namesake. Tell them that you are Imani, and for them to have Faith. Believe," Insect-king instructed Scarab beetle, "with all you hearts in your people, parents, teachers, leaders, and even their children who at times will cause them much pain. Like little streams, they will soon grow in mighty rivers. Remind them of the righteousness of their struggle and neither they, nor their victory must ever be allowed to be underestimated, undervalued, and marginalized. Now go!"

All seven secret messages went out to the ants, but the order they arrived was not the ordered they had been delivered. As with the nature of beetles, though meticulous in nature, they first of all are slow, and secondly, they are very curious creatures. Easily distracted, some ants didn't get any of the Ant-kings secret messages while others maybe the first but not the second, or the third message and not the fourth, and so on and so on. In fact, some of the Ant-king's secret message is still wandering around to this day. The ants who fared worse did not receive any parts of Insect-kings message and to this day many are still awaiting waiting for Insect-king's secret message. In fact, to this very day, Unity, Self-Determination, Collective Work and Responsibility, Collective Economics, Purpose, and Creativity and Purpose only exists among small individual groups. Consequently, ants are always being gobbled up by their enemies.

Something to think about!

Fear and Death

African Proverbs

1. When an enemy digs a grave for you, god gives you an emergency exit. (*Burundi, Rwanda*)
2. If god breaks your leg, he will teach you how to limp. (*Ghana*)
3. Beyond mountains there are more mountains. (Haiti)
4. Blind belief is dangerous. (*Kenya*)
5. Do not follow a person who is running a way. (*Kenya*)
6. When God cooks, you don't see smoke. (*Mozambique, Zimbabwe, Zambia*)
7. Where there is a will there is a way. (*Mozambique, Zimbabwe, Zambia*)
8. A person once bitten by a snake will be scared by an old rope. (*Nigerian*)
9. The power of a crocodile is in the water. (*South Africa*)
10. That which is good is never finished. (*Tanzania*)
11. Anticipate the good so that you may enjoy it. *(unknown)*
12. He who conceals his disease cannot expect to be cured. *(unknown)*
13. He who is bitten by a snake fears a lizard. *(unknown)*
14. He, who is free of faults, will never die. *(unknown)*
15. If you offend, ask for pardon; if offended, forgive. (Ethiopia)

16. If you try to cleanse others – like soap, you will waste away in the process. *(unknown)*

17. The pillar of the world is hope. *(unknown)*

18. It is better to be loved than feared. *(Senegal, Sierra Leon)*

19. Boulders make stones, stones break boulders. *(unknown)*

20. Dreamers remember their dreams when they are in trouble. *(unknown)*

21. However long the night, the dawn will break. *(unknown)*

22. If you understand the beginning well, the end will not trouble you. *(unknown)*

23. It is only god that saves a cow that has no tail from flies. *(unknown)*

24. Knowledge is not the main thing, but good deed is. *(unknown)*

25. Stars shine brightest in the darkest of times. *(unknown)*

26. Tomorrow is pregnant and no-one knows what she will give birth to. *(unknown)*

27. Unless you call out, who will open the door? (Ethiopia)

28. The rabbit that stays in a hole must be ready to face the hunter's fire. *(unknown)*

29. The pants of today are better than the breeches of tomorrow. *(West Africa)*

30. A chicken's prayer doesn't affect a hawk. *(West and Central Africa)*

31. After hardship comes relief. (*West and Central Africa*)

32. There is no bad patience. (*West and Central Africa*)

33. Hope does not kill. (*Zulu*)

34. A knife does not fear thorns, a woman fears man. (*Mongo proverb*)

35. Fear is no obstacle to death. (*West African*)

36. Fear a silent man. He has lips like a drum. (*Yoruba*)

37. Who created thunder does not fear it. (*Burundi*)

38. You don't tie up a good goat to a bad goat. (*Burundi*)

39. No man fears what he has seen grow. (*Egypt*)

40. Tomorrow belongs to the people who prepare for it today. (*Egypt*)

41. The only active force that arises out of possession is fear of losing the object of possession. *Egyptian Proverb*

42. Men fear danger, women, only the sight of it. (Ethiopia)

43. No one knows what the dawn will bring. (Ethiopia)

44. Know those who are faithful to you when you are in low estate. (*Ptah-Hotep*)

45. That which is said in your heart, let it be realized by springing up spontaneously. (*Ptah-Hotep*)

46. To agree to have dialogue is the beginning of a peaceful resolution. (*Somali*)

47. The stream knows where to flow. (Tanzania)

48. If you really love something, your fate is in its hands. (*Tupuri proverb*)

49. Anything with an end must have had a start. *(unknown)*

50. The man who waits for a perfect opportunity, will wait a life-time. (*Yoruba*)

The Tortoise and the Hare (A West African Folktale)

One hot and sunny day, as Hare usually did when he wasn't playing tricks on someone, was boasting about how fast he could run. Well, tired of Hare's boasting, Tortoise declared, "I bet I can beat you in a race." Hare was stunned for a minute. He wasn't sure he heard Tortoise correctly. "Did you say something about a race?" Hare asked. Tortoise elaborated, "I challenge you to a race and I want all the animals present to witness your defeat."

Hare started to laugh, "This is the most ridiculous thing I have ever heard. It will take you many years to cover the distance I can run in one day. It is silly to race against you. Everyone knows that I will win."

"Maybe so," Tortoise said with confidence, "but I challenge you just the same." Well, this went on until Hare agreed to the race so everyone could see how silly Tortoise was and how great and magnificent, he, himself was.

The day of the race, the entire animal kingdom came to witness it. When the race began and Hare bounded away, eager to get the race over with, he still thought it was ridiculous to be competing against Tortoise. What Hare didn't know was that Tortoise had positioned his cousins along the race path while Tortoise himself waited near the finish line. As Hare turned the corner around the forest path, he saw Tortoise walking ahead of him. "This is impossible!" he exclaimed. "How did you get here so fast?"

"Though I walk slowly, when I run fast, I run so fast you don't even see me pass you" Tortoise replied.

"Impossible!" muttered Hare as he ran past Tortoise even faster. Yet, as he turned another corner in the forest path, there again was Tortoise, lumbering ahead of him. "You've got to be kidding me!" said Hare as he approached Tortoise. "How did you get in front of me again?"

"Though I walk slowly, when I run fast, I run so fast you don't even see me pass you" Tortoise replied without breaking his slow and steady gate.

Fear and Faith

"Impossible!" muttered Hare as he ran past Tortoise even faster than before. This went on for several country miles until Hare had run out of both speed and energy. With the finish line in sight, and Tortoise nowhere around, Hare decided to take a much needed nap. In fact, the best he could have done anyway was crawl over the finish line. With his boastful pride on the line, Hare was certainly not going to do that. Again, for good measure he looked behind and in front of him to make sure Tortoise was not even in sight. Seeing that he wasn't, Hare found a nice, cool spot under an acacia tree and fell fast asleep.

Well, the roar of the crowd woke Hare up. "Oh no, this cannot be happening!" he cried as Tortoise neared the finish line. With a bolt, Hare got to his feet and shot toward the finish line. However, as fast as he ran, like a bolt of lightning really, he was a hair short behind the slow and steady Tortoise. "Impossible! Impossible!" Hare shouted out of breath. "Simply impossible!" he shouted as Tortoise was declared the winner of the race. With his arm raised in the air, Tortoise had only one thing to say to his good friend, which was, "Slow and steady wins a race my friend. It is not given to the swift nor the strong, but he who endures until the end."

Something to think about!

Chapter 10 – Love Lines

A Man, His Son, and a Cow (A Fulani Folktale)

There was once a father whose wife had died and left him with three sons and a precious cow who gave birth to a healthy calf every year. One day the father asked his eldest son to take the cow out to graze. Doing as his father asked, the son took the cow to the greenest of fields. After the cow grazed to her content, the son led it to a water-hole so she could drink as long as she desired. Later that evening, when the father asked the cow how she had grazed, the cow complained that she did not have enough to eat. Rubbing her stomach, the cow complained, "Your wicked son took me to a barren patch of earth where no grass grows. Then he tied me up and went to sleep."

After hearing the cow's tale, the angry father sent his eldest son away from home and out into the wilderness. Tearfully, the eldest son wandered until he came upon a small farmhouse where he met a kind farmer. The farmer who also had no wife, and no son either, took the man's eldest son in as his own son. The farmer taught the son how to farm in the winter, spring, summer and fall. The farmer taught the man's eldest son how to farm during feast and famine and everything he knew about farming. As the years went by the farmer said to the boy, "One day I will have to send you back to your father, so you can teach him how to farm. Then he can depend less on that old, wicked cow."

Meanwhile, the father had called to his second son. "My son," he spoke sternly to the youth, "go and graze the cow. She must be well fed and washed." As did the eldest son, the middle child took the wicked cow to the green fields where she grazed until her belly swung low to the ground. Then, he gave the cow a warm bath and tethered her to a tree so she could dry. While the son waited for the cow to dry, he dozed off to sleep. While he was sleeping the father came to check on his prized cow. "Have you eaten?" the father asked the cow. "How could I?" the cow replied. "Your wicked son took me to the most barren of fields where there was little grass, and what little there was, was bitter to the taste. Then," the cow complained, "as you can see, the ungrateful child tied me up and went off to sleep." Upon hearing the cow's story, the father grew angry. He grabbed a big stick and woke his son up with a 'whack' on the leg. The father then chased his second son away from home.

It came to pass that the second son wandered in the wilderness until he came to the house of a blacksmith. The blacksmith, upon hearing the middle child's story, taught him how to combine fire and water to make all sorts of farming and hunting tools. One day, upon admiring a beautiful strung bow that the second son had fashioned, the blacksmith told the boy, "Eventually, I will have to send you back to your father so you can teach him how to make these tools. Then your father can depend less on that wicked cow and learn to love you more as the fine son you are." Nodding, the second son understood, while also continuing to learn from the blacksmith.

Well now, the father was down to his youngest and most favored son. "Go," he spoke kindly to the boy, "and graze the cow. Be sure to take good care of her for it will break my heart to send you away like your brothers." Obedient, as had been his older brothers, the third and youngest son took the cow to the green fields where she grazed and bathed. Then, the most favored son tied his father's cow to the tree so that she could dry and not run off. No sooner had the youngest son sat down to rest did his father come along. "Cow", he asked, "did you have enough to eat?" As the wicked cow had done twice before, she complained of her treatment. "Your favorite son is just as wicked as his two other brothers. He took me to the wilderness where no grass grows, and then he tied me up here to die."

The father was enflamed after listening to the wicked cow's fib. The harsh treatment to his prized and precious cow by his most favored and final son brought tears to the father's eyes. Though he suspected the cow might not be telling the total truth, the father ran his third and most favored son off as he had done his other sons. No amount of pleading from the youngest son could dissuade the father. Days and days the young boy wandered in the wilderness until reaching the house of a great scholar. Mentored by the scholar, the youngest son learned to read and write and orate and debate. At some point, the boy's wise mentor said to him, "Son, although I have taken you in as my own, one day I will have to let you go back to your father. At that time he will know and love you and have been done with that wicked cow."

Over the years, the lonesome father grew grey, wiry and weak. Without the help of his three sons, the father took to grazing his precious cow himself. Much had changed with the boys gone. The farm was falling down around him and his precious cow had even stopped bearing at least one calf a year for him to take to the market. Still, every day the father took his prized cow out to pasture. There, she ate plenty of lush grass and drank plenty of sparkling water. While the father dozed under a tree, the cow was left to dry tethered to a tree.

One warm, sunny, spring morning, after grazing and washing the cow, and after his own nap, the father and asked the cow was she full. To the father's surprise, the cow laughed. "You are a hypocrite like your sons, sir. You took me into the wilderness. You gave me no food and no water. Then you ask me if I'm full? Ha!" Of course, the father couldn't believe his ears. Finally he put it all together. "You have been lying to me all along," he shouted at the cow. "Oh, how stupid of me. I sent my three sons away because of your lies." Before the cow could speak another lying word, the father picked up a big stick and beat the cow until she died.

It took a while for the father to get over loosing not only his three sons, but his precious cow as well. With saddened heart, he set out to find his boys. After so many years had passed, he only hoped that they would not pass him on the road with neither recognizing the other. The father wandered from village to village looking for his sons. For many years he wandered with no luck, returning home heartbroken and more tired and feeble than when he had first set out.

Well, it came to pass on one particular fine and sunny day, the father decided to go to the village market to get a few tools to cook with and a few vegetables to make a pot of stew. Old and thin, while holding a melon in his hand, the father fainted. Villagers came from everywhere to help the old man who had feinted. The first to reach the man was the father's eldest son, who had come to sell some of his farm produce at the market. Trailing only a step or two behind was the second son, who had come to sell the tools he had made. On the heels of the second son came the third, and the farmer's most favored son. The youngest son had come to the market to trade an Anansi story for something of value. Though the boys had not laid eyes on each other in years they recognized each on first sight, the man's three sons immediately recognized their father.

Overjoyed, the boys hugged each other and then immediately attended to their sick father. Upon being reunited with his three sons, a little strength returned to the father's weak and wiry body. With tears in his eyes, he apologized to his sons for believing that old, wicked cow, who he told them, he had beaten to death once having found out the truth. Asking their forgiveness, the father pleaded for his sons to return home with him. "My sons," he told them, "you are more precious than any cow. I have learned that misfortunes, springing from myself, are the hardest to bear."

Something to think about!

Love Lines

African Proverbs

1. What one desires is always better than what one has. (*Ethiopia Proverb*)

2. If love is a sickness, patience is the remedy. (*Cameroonian Proverb*)

3. A beautiful thing is never perfect. (*Egypt Proverb*)

4. A fish and bird may fall in love but the two cannot build a home together.*(unknown)*

5. Pretend you are dead and you will see who really loves you. (*Bamoun Proverb*)

6. He who loves the vase also loves what grows inside. *(unknown)*

7. The word that loves you stays in the belly. (*Burundi Proverb*)

8. It's better to fall from a tree and a break your back than to fall in love and break your heart. *(unknown)*

9. Love is a painkiller. *(unknown)*

10. Love is like cough you can't hold it back. *(unknown)*

11. Love never gets lost, it's only kept. *(unknown)*

12. There is no physician who can cure the disease of love. *(unknown)*

13. To be able to love other people you must be able to love yourself. *(unknown)*

14. To love that one who never loves you is like rain falling in the forest. *(unknown)*

15. True love means what's mine is yours. *(unknown)*

16. A shepherd does not strike his sheep. *(Nigerian Proverb)*

17. Why take away something by force which you can obtain by love. *(unknown)*

18. Perhaps you do not understand me because you do not love me. *(unknown)*

19. He who doesn't feel jealousy is not in love. *(unknown)*

20. Lovers do not hide their nakedness. *(Congolese Proverb)*

21. If the full moon loves you, why worry about the stars? *(Tunisian Proverb)*

22. Love and let the world know, hate it n silence. *(Egyptian Proverb)*

23. The heart is a locket that does not open easily. *(Duala Proverb)*

24. The one who loves an unsightly person is the one who makes them beautiful. *(unknown)*

25. A loved one has no pimples. *(Kenyan Proverb)*

26. Talking with one another is loving one another. *(Kenyan Proverb)*

27. Let your love be like the misty rain, coming softly, but flooding the river. *(Liberian & Madagascan Proverb)*

28. If love is torn apart you cannot stitch the pieces together again. (*Malagasy Proverb*)

29. Let your love be like drizzle: it comes softly, but still swells the river. (*Malagasy Proverb*)

30. Love is just like rice — plant it elsewhere and it grows. (*Malagasy Proverb*)

31. Love is like young rice: transplanted, still it grows. (*Malagasy Proverb*)

32. To agree to have dialogue is the beginning of a peaceful resolution. (*Somali Proverb*)

33. Love is like a rice plant; transplanted, it can grow elsewhere. (*Madagascan proverb*)

34. He may say that he loves you, wait and see what he does for you. (*Senegalese Proverb*)

35. Happiness requires something to do, something to love and something to hope for. (*Swahili Proverb*)

36. The best part of happiness lies in the secret heart of a lover. (*Ugandan Proverb*)

37. Loving someone that does not love you is like loving the rain that falls in the forest. (*West Africa Proverb*)

38. Woman without man is like a field without seed. (*Ethiopia Proverb*)

39. The old woman looks after her hens and the hens look after the old woman. (*Ghana Proverb*)

40. Where there is love there is no darkness. (*Burundian Proverb*)

41. One who plants grapes by the road side, and one who marries a pretty woman, share the same problem. (*Ethiopia Proverb*)

42. When an only cola nut is presented with love, it carries with it more value than might otherwise be associated with a whole pod of several cola nuts. (*Nigerian Proverb*)

43. You know who you love, but you can't know who loves you. (*Nigerian Proverb*)

44. Don't try to make someone hate the person he loves, for he will still go on loving, but he will hate you. (*Senegalese Proverb*)

45. One who marries for love alone will have bad days but good nights. (*Egyptian Proverb*)

46. You only make a bridge where there is a river. (*Luyia, Western Kenya Proverb*)

47. Only someone else can scratch your back. (*Luyia, Western Kenya Proverb*)

48. Your mother is still your mother, though her legs may be small. (*Malawi Proverb*)

49. The quarrel of lovers is the renewal of love. (*Moroccan Proverb*)

50. Where a river flows, there is abundance. (*Nilotic Proverb*)

Fur and Feathers

The pride and joy of Momma Ostrich were her two baby chicks. One day, when Momma Ostrich returned home from gathering food for her two dear chicks, she looked and looked for they were nowhere to be found. Imagine her alarm when she noticed lion tracks leading in and out of her home. Fearful, but determined to find her babies, she followed the lion track into the woods where they ended up at the den of Momma Lion.

"What are you doing with my chicks?" cried Momma Ostrich, fearing for her babies' safety. "Return them to me at once!"

"What do you mean your chicks?" Momma Lion growled. "These are my cub, that's plain to see."

"It's not at all plain to see," cried Momma Ostrich. "Those are ostrich chicks you are a lion!"

"Is that so?" snarled Momma Lion. "Then I dare you find any animal at all that will look me in the eye and tell me that these are not my cubs. Do that and I will release them to you," Momma Lion roared ferociously.

Without another word, Momma Ostrich ran off to each and every animal to tell them that she was assembling a meeting to discuss a terrible injustice. When she arrived at the home of Mongoose and told him her sad story, Mongoose thought and thought until he came up with an idea. He told Momma Ostrich to dig a hole under an ant-hill and on the other side make a second exit out. After doing what Mongoose had requested, Momma Ostrich told all the animals to gather around the ant hill, including Momma Lion. When all they had all assembled, Momma Ostrich explained how Momma Lion had kidnapped her dear, sweet little chicks. "Look," she asked each of them, "can't you see they are ostrich chicks and not lion cubs?"

Momma Ostrich did indeed hear a few animals mumble, "Looks like ostrich chicks to me," but when she asked them to come forward and look Momma Lion in the eye, and repeat it, none would. Though the baby chicks looked exactly like a smaller version of Momma Ostrich, none felt brave or foolish enough to point this out to Momma Lion. In fact, each and every one pointed their eyes down to the ground in fear. Even more, one by one when asked, whispered that the little chicks definitely belonged to Momma Lion.

Momma Lion smiled and growled a fearsome, 'thank you' to each animal, while under her breath she promised not to eat them if they took her side. Well, you know each and every animal, did just that, saying how Momma Ostrich's chicks look remarkably like lion cubs. However, when it came to Mongoose's turn, he cried out, "Have you ever seen a Momma Lion with fur have babies that had feathers? Think of what you are saying. Momma Lion has fur! The chicks have feathers! They belong to the ostrich!" Having made his point, no sooner had Mongoose made his announcement, he jumped down the hole under the ant-hill. At once, Momma Lion jumped up and ran right after Mongoose. With her sharp teeth and claws, she tore at the anthill, having no idea that Mongoose had already exited out the other end.

While Momma Lion ripped away at the anthill trying to get at Mongoose, who of course, had long gone, the babies scrambled right up into their mother's open arms. Momma Ostrich and her babies, not to mention the other animals, then slipped away leaving Momma Lion to pace back and forth around the ant-hill hole waiting for Mongoose to come out. And you know what, even to this day, Momma Lions can be seen pacing about the entrance to ant-hills, waiting for a Mongoose to stick its head out. Off in the distance, if you pay attention, you may also notice Momma Ostrich and her babies laughing from a safe distance at her foolishness.

Something to think about!

Chapter 11 – More Folktales

Lazy Lions Have Full Bellies (by Jesse Sharpe)

Once upon a time, there was a boy named Akouso. Although he was a good boy and did his chores, Akouso often wasted away his day daydreaming.

Akouso's father was a great hunter and storyteller. Everyone spoke of him highly because his adventures were many. Akouso was very proud of his father.

Akouso daydreamed all the time. He daydreamed during the dry season and he daydreamed during the rainy season. Closing his eyes, Akouso would often daydream of swimming in a beautiful lake along with the fish.

One moment Akouso would be daydreaming that he was swimming in the village lake along with the fish, and the next moment he saw himself flying in the sky with the eagles. Akouso often daydreamed of outsmarting Anansi the Spider in a battle of wits. More than anything though, Akouso daydreamed of being a great hunter like his father.

Akouso's father was not only a great hunter, he was a magnificent story teller as well. When the day's work was done, many villagers would gather around a large Acacia tree to listen to Akouso's father's exciting tales. Akouso would be among them, but in no time flat he would lapse into daydreaming.

"My son," Akouso's father would chastise in disappointment, "it is the lion who wakes the dreamer, not his mother's sweet voice."

Well, it came to pass that one day while daydreaming, Akousa strayed too far from his village. As luck would have it, he stumbled upon an old lion named Mustafo.

Tsk, tsk, Akouso's tongue clicked excitedly, seeing that Mustafo was fast asleep with his bloated belly. "Oh great Mustafo, you are so sad. Today, I will return home a great hunter, wearing your lion's mane on my shoulders."

Only pretending to be sleep, Mustafo bristled from the boy's boasting.

"Oh, Akouso," he growled to himself, "tender meat is the best meat. If you did not daydream so much, you would know that he who boasts much cannot do much."

Emboldened, Akouso strutted up to Mustafo and drew back his spear.

"Silly, old lion," he snickered, ready to fling the spear into Mustafo's heart, "there is nothing worse than an old fool. You should not have eaten so much that you cannot even defend yourself."

However, before Akouso could fling his spear, Mustafo was leaping into the air. Caught by surprise, Akouso soon found himself knocked to the ground with the old lion standing over the young boy licking his paws. Akouso cried for help, but his daydreaming had taken him a long way from his village and no one heard him.

"The empty wagon rattles does it?" Mustafo snickered. "Clearly you did not listen to your father and my long-time friend. If you had not been daydreaming you would know that the roaring lion kills no game. However, since the instruction of youth is like an engraving in stone, Mustafo chose to teach Akouso rather than eat him."A few swats," Mustafo growled, "should teach you what I have taught my own pups, which is a roaring lion kills no game."

After a few heavy swats to teach Akouso that whoever attempts to ride a lion's back may end up in his stomach, Mustafo let the boy go. Thankful that he did not end up in the lion's belly, Akouso waved goodbye to Mustafo and hurried back to his village.

"So," Akouso's father asked when Akouso arrived looking the worse for wear. "did you fall from the sky dreaming that you could fly? Were you attacked by an angry alligator who thought you were a fish? Or," his father inquired while tending to his son's wounds, "did Anansi the Spider drag you through a prickly briar patch?"

"None of those," Akouso chuckled. "I can only blame it on my boasting and rattling like an empty wagon when I stumbled upon old Mustafo. I forget that the barking dog never captures the quail," he then painfully admitted. "Most of all," Akouso wisely confessed, "I learned that with their sharp teeth and claws, lazy lions with full bellies are still quite dangerous."

"Any other lessons to share?" Akouso's father asked.

"Father," Akouso answered, after giving the question considerable thought, "Mustafo taught me that lazy lions with full bellies only pretend to be sleep. What they are really doing is waiting for someone with their head in the clouds to come along and be their next meal."

Akouso's father was proud of his son. Although Akouso was a bit bruised, he knew that years from now a wiser Akouso would remember this very day and understand that small pains lead to great gains.

Something to think about!

The Monkey Trial (A Nigerian Folktale)

One day two dogs were wandering in the bush and they found some meat. Unable to decide which of them saw it first, each declared to the other, "I saw it first." Though agreeing they should share the meat, they each wanted the larger piece. The two dogs argued and argued and almost fought. Being the best of friends, they decided to take it to the monkey court for a trial.

Upon seeing the monkey, the dogs saluted and told him everything that had happened. However, as soon as the monkey saw them coming, he had decided he was going to have the meat to himself. Each dog claimed he had seen the meat first. The monkey pretended to listening to both sides of the stories. When the friends had finished stating each of their cases, the monkey suggested to them both, "I think that I had better divide the meat for you and have each person take his portion without argument."

The monkey then dividing the meat as he said he would, making sure that one piece was larger than the other piece. Then, noticing the disparity in size, the monkey picked up the larger piece and took a bite of it. Mmm, the meat was good. When he laid down the piece from which he had taken a bite, and then saw that it was the smaller of the two, he explained to the patient dogs that he had to bite yet another piece to make them even.

This went on for bite after bit. While the monkey seemed to be trying hard, yet he could not get the pieces equal. Each time the piece from which he would take a bite would be the smaller of the two. Finally, when the monkey saw that both pieces of meat were so small it did not wet his appetite, he said to the dogs, "Go home. What little meat there is, I will keep for my fee. You shall not taste any of it." Snatching up the remaining two pieces, he then climbed high into the trees laughing at the two dogs that still had no notion of having been tricked. This is how the two dogs lost all their meat and why even to this day, dogs often quarrel over food. If they had been willing to agree between themselves each would have had a nice piece of meat, and certainly would not have relied on a monkey to decide for them.

Something to think about!

The Jackal's Lawsuit (An Ethiopian Tale)

One day Leopard and Jackal went out together to hunt. After Leopard captured one of Man's goats and Jackal one of Man's cow, the drove their prizes home and put them in the field to pasture. Well really, seeing that Jackal's cow was so much larger than his little goat, suddenly Leopard was not so happy with his small catch. Unable to sleep that night, he got up and went out to the pasture where he found that Jackal's cow now having given birth to a calf. Overcome with envy, Leopard took the calf away from the cow and tethered it to his goat. The next morning, Leopard went to Jackal and said, "How lucky I am! This morning I went to the field and what do you think?"

"What," asked Jackal, anxious to hear about some good fortune Leopard might have had. "Do tell, cousin."

"Well," growled Leopard with feigned excitement, "My goat has given birth to a calf!"

"What! That can't be," Jackal snarled, "for a goat can only give birth to a kid."

"Come for the proof," Leopard challenged. Then, he took Jackal out to the field where sure enough, a calf was tethered to his goat.

"Now you can see for yourself I have spoken the truth," Leopard said.

"Since only a cow can give birth to a calf, the calf is mine," Jackal said.

"Do you see the proof and continue to argue?" Leopard argued. "Can't you see the calf with my goat?"

"Yes, I see her," Jackal agreed, "but even if I saw her standing with an elephant, still she would be mine."

Jackal and Leopard argued this way until Leopard slyly said, "Let other be the judge! If any other animal will see things your way Jackal, you may have my calf. However," Leopard asserted, "I am sure they will recognize that justice is on my side!"

Off jackal and Leopard went in search of judges. The first one they found was Gazelle. Gazelle listened first to Jackal and then to Leopard. In the interest of his own life, Gazelle looked at Jackal with his frightened eyes and cleared his throat. "Well," he said, "when I was young it was true that only cows had calves. But times have changed. The world moves on. Now, as you can see, it is possible for goats to have calves. This is my judgment, as Heaven is my witness!"

"You see how it is," Leopard hummed with confidence. "It is clear that the calf is mine." But having only one animal to voice his opinion didn't seem quite fair to Jackal. Suggesting for at least one more opinion, the two continued along the path until they came across Hyena. However, Hyena too was afraid of Leopard. When Jackal was through making his complaint, Hyena said, with an anxious look on his face, "I have come to the conclusion that ordinary goats cannot have calves, but goats that are owned by leopards can. That is my judgment, as Heaven is my witness!"

Not quite convinced, all of the animals followed Leopard and Jackal to where they came upon little Klipspringer, the rock jumping antelope. Klipspringer listened in skittish silence, and before Jackal could even tell his part, Klipspringer said with a learned air, "Once it was the law of all living things that each one should bear only his own kind. Lions bore lions, goats bore goats, and camels bore camels. But the law has been changed. It is now permitted for goats to bear calves. This is the truth, as Heaven is my witness!"

"Since there are no more judges left," announced Leopard, "the calf is clearly mine."

Upon seeing Baboon in the distance, "There is still Baboon," Jackal said. Though losing his patience, Jackal agreed to ask Baboon for his judgment. "Let this be the last and final word," he warned Jackal. Now, Gazelle, Hyena, and Klipspringer followed Jackal and Leopard to the rocky place where they found Baboon turning over stones to get at the ants and grubs. "Judge our case," demanded Leopard with confidence.

Baboon was not entirely pleased with Leopard's brashness, but was no great fried of Jackal's either. With a mind to bite both of their tails off, Baboon yielded to his temptation and stopped looking for ants. Sitting on a big rock, he decided to listen to Leopard and Jackal's story. When Leopard and Jackal concluded their argument, Baboon reflectively folded his huge, hairy arms. By this time, of course, many other animals had gathered around to learn from Baboon's wise council.

After a while, Baboon slowly climbed up on a high rock and looked down upon both Jackal and Leopard. He seemed to mull his decision over in his head for a long time before he said anything. Even then, Baboon said nothing. Instead, he held a small stone in his hand and plucked at it with his fingers.

"Well?" Leopard said impatiently. "You see how it is. What is your verdict?"

"Wait," Baboon said. "Can't you see I am busy?"

"What are you doing?" Leopard asked gruffly. "Busy doing what?"

"I have eaten my meal and now I must play a little music before I judge," Baboon answered.

"Music? What music?" all the animals asked in unison.

"Here, the music I am playing on this instrument!" Baboon replied with irritation. "I am playing my music."

"Ha! He plucks upon a stone!" Leopard ridiculed. "Look what a stupid person we have asked to judge for us! No music can come from a stone!"

"Aha," Baboon announced, looking directly at Leopard, "then, my good fellow, if a calf can come from a goat, surely sweet music can come from a stone?"

Now, Leopard was embarrassed. "Hmm, what lovely music," he said, caught in his own mischievousness. Emboldened, the other animals then shouted, "It is true! It is true! As Heaven is our witness, only a cow can have a calf!"

And so, because the community was united against him, Leopard returned the calf to Jackal. To this day, though they may be in the same vicinity, Jackal and Leopard do not go out hunt together. Of course, Hyena, Klipspringer, and Gazelle are still on the run from Leopard, while Baboon, seated upon his rocky thrown, looks on with amusement.

Something to think about!

The Hunter and His Three Dogs

(A Yoruba Folktale)

Once there was a hunter who had three dogs. Their names were 'Cut to Pieces', 'Swallow Up' and 'Clear the Remains'. He also had a magic flute by which he could call them up and they came. Whenever the hunter went hunting, he left his dogs tied up to a tree in the village. Before leaving however, the hunter always gave instruction to his wife to release his three dogs if they ever become agitated. Having left these instructions to his wife, the hunter told her that he would return in a couple of days. The hunter's wife waved goodbye to her husband, knowing in a few days he would be returning with enough meat to share with the whole village. The skins and bones of whatever animal he killed would be used for such things as ropes, clothing, drums, cooking and sewing tools, and weapons and medicines. The wife was proud of her hunter husband, for he was a good man.

Now, on this particular trip the hunter found that every time he killed an animal and hung it high up on a branch for safe keeping, when he came back to his camp some monster would have eaten all the meat. First he tried hanging the meat, then he tried hiding it in a cave, he even tried putting it in a circle of fire, but each time he came back, the previous day's meat would be gone – even the bones would have been eaten.

Frustrated, after man days away from his wife and village with no meat to bring back to them, the hunter decided to hide and wait in hopes of killing the great beast. He waited for three days, yet the monster never showed herself. On the fourth day, the man while preparing what little meat he had back to his village, shouted insult and obscenities at the monster.

Well, the monster had been hiding in the thick bush outside the man's camp all this time. She had been waiting for the hunter to bring back some fresh meat for her to dine on. Upon hearing the insults hurled at her, she suddenly came rushing into the man's camp. Oh, she was an ugly monster. Her fur flayed in every direction. Shaking her huge, angry body with its many mouths, her razor sharp teeth snapped at the hunter with the intent on cutting him to small, edible pieces. Having never ever seen such a fierce and frightening beast in all his life, the hunter climbed as fast as he could to the top of a great tree. When he was safely out of the monster's reach, the hunter whistled for his dogs.

As it was, the man's dogs, 'Cut to Pieces', 'Swallow Up' and 'Clear the Remains', were both hunger and agitated from being tied up for such a long time anyway. What little meat the man's wife had been sharing had not kept their bellies from grumbling. When they heard the sound of their master's flute, Cut to Pieces', 'Swallow Up' and 'Clear the Remains' broke loose and rushed as quickly as they could in the direction of the flute.

While the hunter waited for his dogs to arrive, the huge, angry beast ate away at the tree that kept him out of her reach. However, each time the she took a huge gash out of the tree, stripping away bark and fruit, he sprinkled magic powder on the great tree and it became whole again. Eventually, the hunter ran out of magic powder and jabs with his spear seemed only to irritate the great beat even more. It came to a point where the great tree was nearly cut. All that was left to happen was for the hunter to fall into the mouth of the monster.

With his feet nearly in reach of the monster's many mouths, the hunter heard the most beautiful sound in all the world. Seemingly out of nowhere 'Cut to Pieces', 'Swallow Up' and 'Clear the Remains', bolted into the open and living up to their names, they cut the animals to pieces, swallowed her up, and completely cleared what was left of her remains. The hunter was happy to see his faithful dogs and he embraced each and every one of them.

That night, as 'Cut to Pieces', 'Swallow Up', 'Clear the Remains', and the hunter slept under the great tree, the monster's sister appeared to the hunter as a most beautiful woman. Though the dogs sniffed at her suspiciously, the hunter quieted them and decided to take the woman home to be his second wife. When they reached the village, the man's first wife was so overjoyed with her husband's safe return, she did not even quibble over having a younger, more beautiful woman in her house. Though she too was suspicious of the woman, she decided to trust her husband's judgment, for he was indeed a good man.

That night, while the hunter and his first wife slept, the monster resumed her hideous form and tried to kill them. As they had done with the monster's sister, 'Cut to Pieces', 'Swallow Up' and 'Clear the Remains' broke loose from their chains and tore the monster to pieces.

Upon hearing the ferocious battle, both hunter and his wife came outside. They were just in time to see the three dogs finish off the hideous monster.

"Oh how stupid of me," the hunter apologized to his wife, "to want a second wife, when in fact, the first was even was even more beautiful and all I needed in the first place?"

"Tsk, tsk," the wife clicked with her tongue "why indeed?"

Something to think about!

More Folktales

Chapter 12 – Animal Folktales and Proverbs

The Cake (A Folktale)

A little boy sat down on the ground in front of his Grandmother and huffed and puffed until she paid him some attention. His grandmother, smiled, and asked, "Grandson, how was your day in school?"

"Grandma," the little boy whines. "Everything went wrong. I did not do well on a test, and I fell down and scraped my knee." When the little boy showed his grandmother the scrapes on his knee, she slowly bent her old body down and kissed it. Immediately, the boy's felt his knee getting better. "Also grandma," the grandson continued, "a mean, old dog chased me for a whole mile, and when Kuliya saw me running, she frowned, saying that I was not brave enough to marry her."

On and on the little boy fretted until his grandmother shushed him by softly patting his healed knee. "I know what you need," she said, reaching in her cupboard. "How about a little snack?" Immediately her grandson's eyes lit up. "Here," she said, passing him the cooking oil, "have some of this."

"Yuck," said the boy.

From the refrigerator, she gave him two raw eggs."

"Yuck," again he frowned. "That's gross, Grandma."

"Would you like some flour then?" his grandmother asked. "Maybe baking soda?"

"Grandma," the boy complained. "All those things are yucky!"

And as grandmothers do, she smiled, and set the sweetest smelling cake on the table in front of her grandson. "Grandson, all those things seem bad by themselves, but when they are put together, in the right way, they make a wonderfully delicious cake!"

Clearly, not understanding, but hungry just the same, the grandson nodded his head and asked for a teaspoon of oil, cup of flour, baking soda, and the two raw eggs.

African Proverb: The elephant paid no attention to the mosquito on its back. *(unknown)* ...or...a mother hen listens to all of her chicks. *(An Original)*

Camel and Cat Proverbs

1. One camel does not make fun of another camel's hump. *(Ghana)*
2. One camel had one hump, another had two, both shared the fate of the ass, which had none. *(An Original)*
3. A camel's nose in a tent is soon followed by his body. *(Egypt)*
4. The barking of a dog does not disturb the man on a camel. *(Egypt)*
5. In the desert, only a fool laughs at the camel's humps. *(An Original)*
6. A cat may go to a monastery, but she still remains a cat. *(Ethiopia)*
7. Each cat has its own roar. *(unknown)*
8. If stretching were wealth, the cat would be rich. *(unknown)*
9. The cat and the dog stopped their fighting when their master died. *(An Original)*
10. The cat is a lion to the mouse. *(unknown)*

11. When the cat's stomach is full, the rat's back is bitter. *(Haiti)*

12. You come with a cat and call it a rabbit. *(Cameroon)*

Cow and Crocodile Proverbs

1. Before you milk a cow tie it up. *(South African)*

2. Cows have no business in horseplay. *(Jamaican)*

3. Her horns are not heavy for a cow. *(Ethiopia)*

4. If you call one cow, you invite the calf. *(An Original)*

5. Nobody holds the cow by its horn while milking it. *(Ethiopia)*

6. The cattle are as good as the pasture in which they graze. *(Ethiopia)*

7. The cow has no owner. *(Massai)*

8. Don't think there are no crocodiles because the water is calm. *(Kenya)*

9. Do not call alligator long mouth till you pass him. *(Jamaican)*

10. Only when you have crossed the river can you say the crocodile has a lump on his snout. *(Ghana)*

11. Mistake an alligator for a log and end up stiff. *(An Original)*

Dog Proverbs

1. A dog knows the places he has buried his food. *(unknown)*

2. A dog that wants to go astray will not wait to listen to the voice of the master. *(unknown)*

3. An experienced dog does not sniff an empty hole. *(unknown)*

4. As the dog said, 'If I fall down for you and you fall down for me, it is playing.' *(unknown)*

5. Beat the dog; wait for its master. *(Haiti)*

6. Better be the head of a dog than the tail of a lion. *(unknown)*

7. Do not respond to a barking dog. *(Morocco)*

8. Don't kick a sleeping dog. *(unknown)*

9. If you stop every time a dog barks, your road will never end. *(Saudi Arabian)*

10. The barking of a dog does not disturb the man on a camel. *(Egyptian)*

11. Those who sleep with dogs will rise with fleas. *(Morocco)*

Elephant and Rhino Proverbs

1. Although the elephant is stronger, we give the stool to the antelope. *(Ghana)*

2. An elephant's tusks are never too heavy for it. *(Zimbabwe)*

3. The body of an elephant follows its nose. *(unknown)*

4. If there were no elephant in the jungle, the buffalo would be a great animal. *(Ghana)*

5. One cannot know the grandeur of an elephant by looking at its tail. *(unknown)*

6. The best way to eat the elephant standing in your path is to cut it up into little pieces. *(unknown)*

7. The elephant will reach to the roof of the house. *(Cameroon)*

8. The bold frog kicks the wounded elephant. *(unknown)*

9. When an elephant steps on a trap, no more trap. *(unknown)*

10. Do not jab a rhinoceros if there is no tree nearby. *(Zulu)*

11. The rhinoceros's single tusk killed two men. *(An Original)*

12. The rhino does not eat meat, but the lion fears her. *(An Original)*

13. The fool who tried to ride a rhino, got rode by the rhino. *(An Original)*

Water Creature Proverbs

1. A crab does not beget a bird. *(Ghana)*

2. As a crab walks, so walk its children. *(unknown)*

3. Don't bargain for fish which are still in the water. *(unknown)*.

4. Fish grow fat for the benefit of the crocodile. *(unknown)*

5. The crab that walks too far falls into the pot. *(Haiti)*

6. The shark being cooked for dinner did not enjoy its morning meal. *(unknown)*

7. Throw a lucky man in the sea, and he will come up with a fish in his mouth. *(Saudi Arabia)*

Fox and Frog Proverbs

1. Hunger will lead a fox out of the forest. *(unknown)*
2. The fox follows its tracks. *(An Original)*
3. When the fox's dinner was stolen, he cried foul. *(An Original)*
4. The fox only calls the lion dumb from a distance. *(unknown)*
5. The frog does not realize the importance of water until the draught. *(unknown)*
6. The frog wanted to be as big as the elephant, and burst. *(Ethiopia)*
7. The frog who jumps into the pot knows there's no fire. *(unknown)*
8. The frog who wanted to be as big as the elephant, ended up under its feet. *(unknown)*

Gazelle and Goat Proverbs

1. Every morning in Africa a gazelle awakens knowing that today it must run faster than the fastest lion. *(unknown)*
2. The gazelle's heart is in its swiftness of foot. *(An Original)*
3. The beautiful gazelle met an ugly death. *(An Original)*

4. A white goat disappears as it is being watched. *(unknown)*

5. The goat that stayed with a donkey learned farting. *(Ethiopia)*

6. The goat which has many owners will be left to die in the sun. *(Haiti)*

Horse and Hyena Proverbs

1. Misfortunes come on horseback and depart on foot. *(unknown)*

2. You can take a horse to water, but you can't make him drink. *(Rwandan)*

3. A hyena intrudes through a gap a dog opened. *(Ethiopia)*

4. Do not give a hyena meat to look after. *(unknown)*

5. Two smells of cooking meat breaks the hyena's legs. *(Kikuyu)*

6. Without its pack, a hyena is just a dog. *(An Original)*

Two Roads Overcame the Hyena (A Folktale)

A very hungry hyena went out on the Tanzanian plains to hunt for food. He came to a branch in the road where the two paths veered off in different directions.

Seeing two goats caught in the thickets at the far end of the two different paths, his mouth watering in anticipation. Excited, he decided that his left leg would follow the left path and his right leg would run along the right path. As the two paths continued to veer off in different directions, the hungry hyena was split in two.

African Proverb: *When given two options, select only one.*

Hen and Chicken Proverbs
1. Chickens do not smell the frying pan, but they run from their own shadow. *(An Original)*
2. The hen with baby chicks doesn't swallow the worm. *(West and Central Africa)*
3. A new hen would always have a string tied to its leg. *(unknown)*
4. The egg shows the hen where to hatch. *(unknown)*
5. You don't buy a hen to rear from the market. *(unknown)*
6. The hen debated the eagle until her chicks were safely in the bush. *(An Original)*

Cock and Rooster Proverbs
1. A country rooster would not crow while in town. *(unknown)*
2. A rooster crows only when he sees the light. *(unknown)*

3. A man may think he is a rooster, but he is not. A man may barely service one hen, much less, ten. *(An Original)*

4. The cock that is drunk is yet to meet the hawk that is irate. *(unknown)*

5. The young cock crows as he hears the old one. *(Yoruba)*

Eagle Proverbs

1. No need to teach an eagle to fly. *(unknown)*

2. The eagle that fell from his nest ran with the chickens until it learned to fly. *(An Original)*

3. The eagle wore the plumes of the peacock. *(An Original)*

4. Teach a chicken to fly, and he will still be eaten by the eagle. *(An Original)*

General Birds Proverbs

1. A bird which eats berries can be caught, but not a bird that eats wood. *(Maaori)*

2. A chattering bird will not build a nest. *(West African)*

3. If you put corn on the ground, birds act like lions. *(An Original)*

4. In a court of fowls, the cockroach never wins his case. *(Rwandan)*

5. The jaybird doesn't rob its own nest. *(West Indian)*

6. The peacock loves peas, but not those that go into the pot with it. *(Wolof)*

Insects Proverbs

1. A termite can do nothing to a stone but lick it. *(Sudanese)*
2. Be your enemy an ant, see in him an elephant. *(Turkey)*
3. Caution is not cowardice; even ants march armed. *(Uganda)*
4. Every beetle is a gazelle in the eyes of its mother. *(Morocco)*
5. In the ant's house, the dew is a flood. *(unknown)*
6. No fly enters a mouth that is shut. *(Ethiopia)*
7. No one sees a fly on a trotting horse. *(unknown)*
8. The busy beetle dug a river, and all the village ate. *(unknown)*
9. The elephant paid no attention to the mosquito on its back. *(unknown)*
10. The leech does not let go even when it is filled. *(unknown)*
11. When spider webs unite, they can tie up a lion. *(Ethiopia)*

Lion Proverbs

1. Almost is not eaten. *(Zulu)*
2. Even a weak lion is not bitten by a dog. *(unknown)*
3. Every beast roars in its own den. *(Bantu)*
4. If you beat a lion, expect to be eaten. *(unknown)*

5. If you spear a lion and only wound it, better not to have speared it at all. *(unknown)*

6. The lion does not turn around when a small dog barks. *(unknown)*

7. The lion is a beautiful animal, when seen at a distance. *(Zulu)*

8. The whisper of a pretty girl can be heard further than the roar of a lion. *(Saudi Arabia)*

Why Lions Chase Gazelles (Folktale)

Every morning in Africa, a gazelle wakes up and it knows it must run faster than the fastest lion or it will be killed. Most mornings, it does just that and lives to see another sunset. Every morning, a lion wakes up in Africa and it knows it must outrun the slowest gazelle or it will starve to death. Every so often it does just that, and lies on its side during sunset enjoying its meal. Some mornings, you will find a lion with a gazelle in its mouth, and some mornings, you won't. Buffaloes, wildebeest, hyenas, warthogs, and monkeys all look on, neither complaining nor celebrating. All knew that their time would come one day too.

African Proverb: Every dog has its day…or… in order to get ahead in life, hit the ground running.

Monkey Proverbs

1. The day a monkey is destined to die, all trees get slippery. *(unknown)*
2. The monkey forgets the tree that caused it to fall into the leopards mouth. *(An Original)*
3. The monkey who befriended the alligator, found friendship fleeting. *(An Original)*
4. The monkey who laughs at the fate of others is soon eaten. *(unknown)*
5. You do not teach the paths of the forest to an old gorilla. *(unknown)*

Mouse Proverbs

1. It is only the earth that knows that a mouse's baby is sick. *(Zimbabwe)*
2. The mouse that makes jest of a cat has already seen a hole nearby. *(Nigeria)*
3. When the mouse squeaks, the cat eats. *(An Original)*

The Community of Mice (Folktale)

Once upon a time there were some mice that lived in an African village. In one particular house there was a very large and mean cat which terrorized the mice. In the spirit of unity they decided to work together and dig a large hole. Though the hole was large enough for all the mice, the entrance was very small. No matter how determined the big, mean cat was, it could not squeeze a single paw into the hole. The cat's frustrated efforts had the community of mice pleased and they applauded their teamwork and cooperation. Drinks were passed around and plenty of food was eaten in celebration. Then, as an afterthought, one of the mice stood up. "*But what if...*" he shouted.

"What if what?" several other mice responded.

"What if," the lone mouse responded, "we leave the hole? The cat can't go into the hole but he surely can still catch us as we enter and leave the hole. Who then is going to tie a bell around the cat's neck to warn us when he is approaching?"

Now, all the mice grew silent. With reason, they were afraid. While they succeeded in building the hole together, not a one was ready to sacrifice themselves to tie the bell around the big, mean cat's tail.

African Proverb: The mouse that makes jest of a cat has already seen a hole nearby. *(Nigeria)*

Mule and Donkey Proverbs

1. An ass is but an ass, though laden with gold. *(unknown)*
2. Honey is not sweet for a donkey. (Ethiopia)
3. The donkey sweats so the horse can be decorated with lace. (Haiti)
4. Whoever plows with a team of donkeys must have patience. *(Zimbabwe)*

Ox and Pig Proverbs

1. The fool who owns an ox is seldom recognized as a fool. *(South Africa)*
2. An ox, a pig, and a mouse smelled fire, the ox trotted from the fire as fast as it could, the mouse tunneled under the fire as far as it could, the pig, well, it sweetened the fire as much as it could. *(An Original)*

3. A warthog eating its fill does not delight a pig. *(Sena)*

4. The hen that pecked at the pig during breakfast lay beside the ham for dinner. *(An Original)*

Porcupine, Rabbit, and Rat Proverbs

1. If you sleep with a porcupine, expect to get stung. *(unknown)*

2. The porcupine's needles are not just for show. *(An Original)*

3. A hare is like an ass in the length of its ears, yet it is not its son. *(West African)*

4. If you chase two rabbits, both will escape. *(unknown)*

5. The boastful rabbit has many escape routes. *(unknown)*

6. The rat cannot call the cat to account. *(unknown)*

7. The mouse trap did not hold the rat. *(An Original)*

Monster in Rabbit's House (A Folktale)

Once upon a time, a rabbit lived in a little house by a river. One day, after paying a visit to his friend, Goat, he returned to find his front door shut and strange tracks on the ground. "Who is in my house?" Rabbit yelled into his house.

"It is I, the eater of rabbits," replied a raspy voice from inside Rabbit's house. "Go away or I will come out and eat you!"

Rabbit was so frightened that he ran away without even bothering to investigate. As he ran, blinded by fear, he bumped into Elephant.

"Rabbit!" Elephant exclaimed, "Why are you in such in hurry this morning?"

"There is a monster in my house!" Rabbit cried.

"Don't be silly," Elephant said. "There are no monsters. I will go and see for myself."

So Elephant went back to Rabbits little house with Rabbit trailing along. When they stopped outside Rabbit's door, with a trumpeting shout, Elephant yelled, "Who is in Rabbit's house?"

"It is I, eater of elephants," a throaty voice croaked in return. "Go away or I will come out and eat you!"

"I think that is the scariest voice I've ever heard," cried Elephant. "There must be a huge monster in your house." And then, with great haste, both he and

Rabbit's ran from the house. As they ran in fear, they Elephant and Rabbit ran into Lion.

"Help us!" cried Elephant. "There is a dreadful monster in Rabbit's house!"

"Come now," said Lion, "There are no such things as monsters. Let's go together and see who is scaring my friends."

After a short walk out of the jungle, all three friends, Elephant, Lion, and Rabbit, stood in front of Rabbit's little house by the river. "Who is in Rabbit's house?" roared Lion.

"It is I, eater of lions!" yelled the monster. "Go away or I will come out and eat you!"

"What?" Lion bellowed. "I am not afraid of you!" Without an ounce of fear, Lion yanked opened Rabbit's front door and to their shock, right there in the middle of the floor, laughing and croaking, sat an old fat frog.

"So," Lion laughed. "you are the dangerous monster that frightened my friends!"

"Yes," I am croaked the frog. "Goes to show you, me a little frog, can roar as loud as you, the mightiest of all animals."

"True," said Lion, before licking his lips.

African Proverb: The frog who croaks the loudest is soon silenced. *(unknown)*

Scorpion and Sheep Proverbs

1. When the scorpion stings you, you sting it. *(unknown)*
2. When the scorpion threatened to sting the baboon, the baboon laughed. *(An Original)*
3. A bleating sheep loses a bite. *(Ethiopia)*
4. As the shepherd sleeps, the sheep creep, and the wolf eats. *(An Original)*
5. While the two princes argued, the sheep became silent. *(unknown)*

Snake Proverbs

1. A kind word can attract even the snake from his nest. *(Saudi Arabia)*
2. Bitten by a snake; frightened of a rope. *(unknown)*

3. Do not walk into a snake pit with your eyes open. *(Somalia)*

4. If a rich man ate a snake, they would say it was because of his wisdom; if a poor man ate it, they would say it was because of his stupidity. *(Saudi Arabia)*

5. The fool used the vipers' head as a cushion. *(An Original)*

6. Use your enemy's hand to catch a snake. *(Egypt)*

7. When the snake is in the house, one need not discuss the matter at length. *(unknown)*

8. Whom a serpent has bitten, a lizard alarms. *(unknown)*

9. Without the head, the snake is nothing but a rope. *(unknown)*

Origin of Death Myth of the Chameleon and the Snake
(A Folktale)

When God had finished creation he wanted to send people an important message. He called Chameleon to go and tell them that after death they will return to life. Well, while on her way, Chameleon stopped off and had lunch with her friend Snake. In those days, snakes and chameleons were the best of friends. After much gossip, tea, and a hefty meal, Chameleon took leave of her friend, Snake. Unfortunately, by the time she got to the people, Chameleon had mixed up God's message to. Instead of informing the people they would have everlasting life, she told them, "After death, there is no return."

Being a message from God, the therefore did not complain when they died. Well, God had a tithy when he found out people were not coming back to life and was very angry with Chameleon. Calling her to him, when she was confronted, Chameleon blamed it all on snake. "If Snake had not stopped me on the way, and confused me with her babble," Chameleon told God, "I would have delivered your message exactly as instructed."

The next day, God confronted Snake. Fearing God, Snake lied as well, saying that she hadn't seen her friend, Chameleon. Now, truly furious, God grabbed Snake by her tail and was going to bash her head with a rick. Fearing for her life, Snake quickly crawled out of her own skin before God could get a good grip. To this day snakes still can be found hiding under rocks and shedding their skin.

As for Chameleon, to this day she camouflages herself in an attempt to hide from God. But it a tough task to hide from God, who always finds you. It is almost as hard to hide from the people, who are looking for you too. And then there are all of Snakes friends, like lizards and birds of prey. Nowadays, Chameleon spends the better part of her day in hiding for fear of being a part of their tasty stew.

African Proverb: To discover truth, one must encounter falsehoods. *(Egypt)*

Tiger and Wolf Proverbs

1. A tiger does not have to proclaim its tigritude. *(Nigeria)*
2. Do not blame God for having created the tiger, but thank Him for not having given it wings. *(unknown)*
3. He who rides a tiger is afraid to dismount. *(Nigeria)*
4. The child of a tiger is a tiger. *(Haiti)*
5. Live with wolves, and you learn to howl. *(Morocco)*
6. The white wolf amongst the sheep could not conceal its nature. *(An Original)*
7. Wolves can quiet their stomachs, but their eyes reveal themselves. *(An Original)*

8. When lions and wolves go out hunting, wolves come back famished. *(An Original)*

The Lion's Share (A Folktale)

One day the lion, the wolf and the dog went out hunting together. They caught a wild ass, a gazelle and a hare. The lion spoke to the dog, who seemed to be a bright fellow. "Mr. Dog, you may divide the catch." To this, the dog replied, "I am honoured my king. I think it best that you should have the ass and my friend, the wolf, should take the hare. As for me, I shall be content to take only the gazelle." On hearing this, with a mighty swipe of his claw, the lion struck cracking open the dog's skull.

Turning to the wolf, "Now you may try and divide our meal better," the lion roared. The wolf, who quickly sized up the situation, spoke solemnly, "The ass will be your dinner, my King, the gazelle will be Your Majesty's supper, and the hare, well, it will be your breakfast tomorrow morning." Surprised, the lion asked, "When did you attain so much wisdom?" Stepping back, the wolf answered smartly, "When I heard the dog's skull cracking."

African Proverb: The dog only calls the lion dumb from a distance. *(An Original)...or...*What is taken for oneself is usually not a small piece. *(Ethiopia)*

Animal Folktales and Proverbs

Activities and Lesson Planning

All stories have a purpose. This is no different with folktales and proverbs. The following activities are suggested to help bring about greater appreciation and understanding of the many proverbs and folktales you have read in this book.

1. Read with an awareness of geography (i.e. location and settings).
2. Notice or pick out cultures themes or traditions.
3. Identify themes in folktales represented by the stories and connecting them with the folktale or expression (examples):

    ☐ How Things Start (Creation, Conflicts, etc.)

    ☐ Minding your own business

    ☐ Compassion

    ☐ Greed and Stinginess

    ☐ Pride and Honor

    ☐ Trust and Respect

    ☐ Importance of Family or Tradition

    ☐ Cleverness/Stupidity

    ☐ Consequences of One's Actions

    ☐ Listening to Elders

4. Explain or discuss the oral tradition and compare it to how important information is taught in today's society.

5. Recognize and describe valued or shunned character traits.

6. Explain the use of nature and animals in the teaching of important lessons.

7. Explain the lesson or moral of each folktale or proverb.

8. Describe the special characteristics of the people or animals in the folktales.

9. Using a map of Africa, locate the country or region of the expressions and folktales.

10. Create, write, or orate your own folktales and proverbs.

11. Explain in your own words the definition of a proverb (description).

12. Explain in your own words the definition of a folktale (description).

13. Define culture and tradition, and how it might relate to a particular folktale or proverb.

14. Make paper machete masks and wear traditional African clothing while acting out a folktale. (A good idea would be

to videotape the performance and post it on the family or school web page.)

15. Invite a griot (storyteller) to class or to your community center.

16. Create vocabulary from the folktales and/or proverbs.

17. Research the culture of the various African countries or ethnic groups.

18. Create a word search or crossword puzzle using vocabulary words and themes from the proverbs and folktales.

19. Compare African folktales and expressions with those of other countries or ethnicities.

20. Compare African folktales and proverbs with African American folktales.

21. Define and discuss the following key phrases occurring in the book's Introduction:

   ☐ reinforcing cultural traditions

   ☐ group identity and homogeneity

   ☐ artistic communication

   ☐ native language

- ☐ generation to generation

- ☐ the fabric of African culture

- ☐ political and social stances

- ☐ moral teachings/instructions

- ☐ life experiences

- ☐ universal wisdom

- ☐ political overtones

- ☐ common expression

- ☐ falsely malign

- ☐ coded message

- ☐ beliefs and practices

Activities & Lesson Planning

References

References

African folktales and parables can be found on the internet as well as in many books. Listed below are just a few internet sources from which these and other stories and proverbs may be found. I've also included a short bibliography of books relating for the book collectors.

Note: With the information and websites constantly changing, some of the links listed below may no longer be working. At the same time, since this book has been published, many, many more are probably available.

The Meaning of Ase (Ah Shey)

Ase is a Yoruba word and concept meaning, power, command, authority, and infused with the ability "to make things happen" or "produce change." Ase also refers to the spiritual life force that flows through all living things. Often the salutation to a narrative, speech, or prayer, it also means "let it be so" or "so be it."

Some Popular Internet Sources

African Tales

http://ccs.clarityconnect.com/NRiggs/AfricanFolktales.html

http://ocean-anaedo.org/Proverbs.aspx

Afritopic: http://www.afritopic.com/afritopic-proverbs.htm

http://www.special-dictionary.com/proverbs/

South African Folktales by James A. Honeÿ, M.D.,
http://www.sacred-texts.com/afr/saft/index.htm

Nelson Mandela's Favorite Folktales:
http://www.mandelasfavoritefolktales.com/

Folktales from West Africa: http://allfolktales.com/folktales.php

African Proverbs Sayings and Short Stories:
http://www.afriprov.org/

References

African Proverbs

http://cogweb.ucla.edu/Discourse/Proverbs/African.html

World of Quotes:
http://www.worldofquotes.com/proverb/African/1/index.html

Wikipedia: http://en.wikiquote.org/wiki/African_proverbs

World of Folktales: http://worldoftales.com/

https://www.msu.edu/user/hamza/BuraFolktales.htm

Lesson Plans and Instructions

http://www.yale.edu/ynhti/curriculum/units/1993/2/93.02.05.x.html

African Folktales and Fables: Lesson Plans for Teachers:
http://africa.mrdonn.org/fablelessons.html

http://teacherlink.ed.usu.edu/tlresources/units/byrnes-africa/aindex.htm#African Folktales

LitPlans: Lesson Plan folklore-and-mythology:
http://litplans.com/authors/_Lesson_Plan_folklore-and-mythology.html

Bibliography

One hundred and twenty-five African parables & wise Proverbs, Josiah N. Nwaogwugwu

Parables and Fables: Exegesis, Textuality, And Politics In Central Africa, by V. Y. Mudimbe

Once upon a Time in Africa: Stories of Wisdom and Joy, by Joseph G. Healey (Editor)

African Proverbs and Proverbial Names, by Jonathan Musere (Translator)

Abiyoyo: Based on a South African Lullaby and Folk Story, by Pete Seeger

Zomo the Rabbit: A Trickster Tale from West Africa (ABR), by Gerald McDermott

Nelson Mandela's Favorite African Folktales, by Nelson Mandela (Editor)

Village of Round and Square Houses, by Ann Grifalconi

The Hero with an African Face: Mythic Wisdom of Traditional Africa, by Clyde W. Ford

References

Sunjata: A West African Epic of the Mande Peoples (New Edition), by David C. Conrad (Translator)

The Girl Who Married a Lion: And Other Tales from Africa, by Alexander McCall Smith

The Signifying Monkey: A Theory of African American Literary Criticism, by Henry Louis Gates, Jr.

African Proverbs: Wisdom of the Ages, by Abdulai, David.

Swahili proverbs. Proverbium in cooperation with the African Studies Program, University of Vermont, by Knappert, Jan

*African and Afro-American Proverb Parallel*s. Dissertation, by Campbell, Theophine Maria

Proverbs: Window on the Xhosa World, by Neethling, S. J.

The Poetry of African American Proverb Usage: A Speech Act Analysis, by Dennis W. Folly

*Kinds of Relationships in Igbo Proverbs Usage. Africana Marburgensi*a, by Ambrose A. Monye

On Why People Use Proverbs, by Ambrose A. Monye

32849116R00118

Made in the USA
Middletown, DE
11 January 2019